D1467839

The Crown of Ilyor

Annie Cribbs

Cover illustration and design by Benjamin Wood.

Illustrations by Emma Wood and Rebecca Roeser. Calligraphy by Jeanne Roeser.

Copyright © 2023 by Annie Cribbs

Paperback ISBN: 978-1-962906-04-3

Hardback ISBN: 978-1-962906-03-6

Ebook ISBN: 978-1-962906-01-2

All rights reserved.

No portion of this book may be reproduced in any form without written permission from the publisher or author, except as permitted by U.S. copyright law.

To Jesus, for transforming painful things into beautiful gems.

Contents

Chapter One

Mondays

A warm breeze gently blew a strand of curly, red hair across Charlotte's face. She closed her eyes and turned toward the sun. Sometimes she felt as though she needed the warmth of the sun more than a flower needed it to grow. She loved this time of year. It was early June, and colorful flowers were blooming in gardens, bright green leaves covered tree limbs, and the weather was perfectly mild. It was just before the sticky heat of summer set in.

After soaking up as much light as she could, she flipped her kickstand up, hopped on her bike, and rode down the driveway toward Mary's house. Mary lived a few houses down, on the opposite side of the street. She and Charlotte had been best friends ever since Charlotte moved to Virginia at the start of second grade. Now, three years later, they were practically inseparable. One of the things Charlotte liked best about Mary's house was the blue and cream-colored shutters, which reminded her of the beach.

She parked her bike in the driveway and skipped up the stone pathway. She walked in without knocking and kicked her shoes into the pile. Mary's mom, Mrs. Albright, peeked her head out from the kitchen and smiled.

"Hey, you. Come try a cookie; it's a new recipe." She winked before ducking back behind the wall.

Baking was one of Mrs. Albright's favorite things to do, and the smell of her house always made Charlotte's mouth water. Charlotte grabbed a few cookies from the tray and sat down. Swinging her feet absent-mindedly, she kicked the bar underneath her chair and dunked the cookie in a glass of milk. Mary walked in and giggled when she saw the milk mustache on her friend's mouth.

"I think these are my favorite so far," Charlotte mumbled with her mouth full.

"You say that every time." Mary laughed and grabbed a cookie for herself.

Mary was slightly taller than Charlotte and had straight brown hair and freckles. She had recently confided in her friend that she sometimes wondered if she was adopted since no one else in her family had freckles. She envied her sister, Katherine, whose complexion was clear and un-speckled.

After munching the cookies, Mary hopped up and gave her mom a side hug. "I think Dad will love these."

Mr. Albright, or Mr. A, was the reason Charlotte knew Mary wasn't adopted. Not only did they share the same nose, but Mr. Albright was one of the smartest people she knew, and Mary was just like him.

The girls headed out the back door, running to the steep slope behind the house. Mr. Albright had tied a rope swing to a large branch right near the edge of the drop-off. Charlotte grabbed the cord and swung out with a holler. Mary always got goosebumps when Charlotte swung over the edge like that. She preferred to keep her own feet flat on the ground. Landing in just the right spot, Charlotte chased Mary down the hill, pulling on branches along the way for support.

At the bottom, they trekked over fallen leaves that covered the ground from last fall while they each carried a long stick, watching carefully for Copperheads. They'd only come across one once before, but it was scary enough to make Mary extra cautious, and exciting enough for Charlotte to hope to see another.

Charlotte was always happiest in the woods; it was cool and peaceful. More importantly, there were no new siblings to worry about. When they came to their favorite spot, Mary followed Charlotte around the roots of a fallen tree, using the trunk to cross the creek. The thunderstorms from the week before had filled the stream, so they spent the afternoon catching minnows and chasing water bugs.

When it was time to go home, Charlotte dropped the stick she was using and dried her hands on her jeans. They trudged back up the hill slowly, savoring the last of the day. "Tomorrow after church?" Charlotte said when it was time to part ways.

"See you then," Mary replied.

That night, Charlotte felt restless. She lay in bed tossing and turning. No matter how much she tried, the knot in her stomach wouldn't go away. Letting out a sigh, she turned to face the wall. With all the unfamiliar things in her room, she figured it might help not to look at them.

But she still knew they were there.

Not even her own room felt peaceful anymore. Rolling onto her back, she flicked on the light. The brightness blinded her before her eyes could adjust. When they did, she wished they hadn't. The large white crib sat on what was her soon-to-be new sister's half of the room. She wasn't sure how she felt about it exactly, but she was pretty sure she didn't like it.

Her mom was pregnant with another girl. A *baby* girl. She already knew the baby would get all of the attention. A girl in school had a baby brother last year and said it seemed like all her parents did was take care of the baby.

Charlotte had grown up as the only girl in the family with two older brothers. She'd always been her daddy's little girl. She worried *that* might change too. Her parents had assured her they'd still love her just as much, but she didn't feel special anymore. The new baby would be special.

She blew out another sigh. The only thing that took her mind off the idea was when she played outside with Mary. Sometimes she'd imagine they were different people exploring far-off places away from baby bottles and preoccupied parents. She dreamt of finding a place where she didn't have to give up part of her room and was still her daddy's *only* little girl. She longed for things to go back to the way they were. And even though they would play outside again tomorrow, the weekends always seemed to go by too fast.

Sure enough, Monday morning came too soon, and she found herself sitting at her desk trying to pay attention. This year, the girls were in the same fourth-grade class at Bunson Elementary. Their teacher, Mrs. Harding, was a tall, thin woman with short brown hair and glasses which slipped down her nose when she spoke. She was stricter than most teachers, but Charlotte liked her, even if she would never let Mary and her sit together.

Today, however, Charlotte was in no mood for learning. Mrs. Harding was lecturing the class on the importance of being respectful to their peers. All because Tommy Jones had put a worm in Stacey Willcott's hair during recess. Neither Stacey nor her friends would dare touch a bug, so Stacey stood there shrieking until one of the teachers pulled it out. Mrs. Harding was very upset when she heard what happened, and now the whole class had to suffer.

Charlotte sat doodling in her notebook, trying not to snicker about a little worm causing so much trouble. She glanced at Mary who was nodding her head attentively. After writing a quick note, she tore the paper from her notebook as quietly as possible and crumpled it into a ball. As Mrs. Harding turned to the board to begin the lesson, Charlotte threw it.

Mary jumped when it hit her in the head. She glared over at Charlotte, who smiled innocently.

Uncrumpling the page, it read: *Come to my house after school?* Shaking her head, Mary began to write. She held it up for Charlotte to see.

Family Meeting.

Charlotte groaned. Mrs. Harding turned and peered at her over her glasses. Grimacing, Charlotte sank into her chair. Only one more week of school and she could hardly wait for summer vacation.

While they walked to the bus afterward, Mary explained that her parents had to meet with someone about a property. Charlotte made a face.

"But why do you have to go?"

"I don't know," she sighed. "My dad says it's a family matter. But you can come over as soon as I get back."

It was nearly five o'clock before Charlotte went skipping down the street to Mary's house. The sun lingered in the sky later than normal, allowing Charlotte to stay out a bit longer. The promise of summer hung in the air and she relished the freedom it would bring.

Slowing to a walk, she wondered about Mary's family meeting. *What was so important that Mary had to be there? What property did they have to see?* She puzzled over this until a startling thought popped into her head. *What if the Albrights were planning to move?* Mary's dad had mentioned the house for sale on the corner of Westbury. That would be too far for Charlotte to visit each day on her bike. *What if Mary finds another best friend- a friend who lives closer?*

Her stomach tightened as her thoughts jumbled together, leaving no room for reason. It would be one thing to lose having her own room, but it'd be much worse to lose her best friend. In her flurry of thinking, she didn't realize she'd begun walking faster and was now nearly running toward Mary's house.

As she made her way up the driveway, her legs felt like lead. She burst through the front door. Bounding up the stairs, she said a quick hello to the surprised Mrs. Albright and turned down the hall. She had to hear from Mary herself whether or not she was moving.

When she threw open the door, a startled Mary looked up and said, "Well, hello. You got here fast."

Charlotte realized she'd been a bit hasty storming into the room but she got right to the point. "Are you moving to the house on the corner of Westbury that your dad said he liked on the way home from school last week?" The words tumbled out faster than she meant for them to.

Mary's eyebrows scrunched up in confusion. "We're not moving anywhere."

Charlotte breathed a sigh of relief and fell onto the bed dramatically. "I'm so glad to hear you say that. I thought that's what your meeting was about."

"Oh, that? No, that was just about an old house my dad's uncle left him in his will. We checked it out. My mom said it gives her the creeps, and my dad said it's so old it's not worth anything," she said, tying off the braid in her hair and adjusting her glasses in the mirror.

"An old house?" Charlotte was intrigued. "Sounds exciting."

Mary sat on the edge of her bed. "Not really. It looked like it was about to fall over."

Charlotte thought for a minute but decided to drop the subject.

"Do you want some dinner? I think we're having pizza," Mary asked.

Charlotte's stomach growled.

"I take that as a 'yes'."

When they walked into the kitchen, they found Mary's older sister, Katherine, sitting at the table examining her nails. "Hey, Char, what's up?" She glanced over at her before choosing a bright pink nail polish.

"Not much," Charlotte said as she plopped down next to her and watched her run a smooth coat of paint over each fingernail. She looked at her own ragged nails and wondered why people fussed over them. She had let Mary paint her toes at a birthday party last month, but she couldn't be bothered to do them herself. They'd just get messed up making mud pies anyway. She liked Katherine though, even if she didn't understand her.

Mr. Albright set the food on the table and sat down. "I hope you girls are hungry."

Charlotte's mouth was watering. The Albright's pizza was even better than take-out. She put three pieces on her plate.

"Save some for the rest of us." He laughed, glancing over at her.

She smiled back at him. She loved feeling as comfortable with Mary's family as she did her own. Enjoying every bite, she listened as Mary's parents talked more about the mysterious old house.

When Mrs. Albright asked her husband what he intended to do with it, he brushed off the topic as if it were an irritating fly. "I have to look more closely at the will, but I'll probably have it demolished and sell the property. No sense in keeping something we don't need."

Charlotte thought it was a shame to destroy something that seemed so intriguing.

After clearing the table, the girls ran to get their shoes on. "Race you to the fort," Mary said.

Charlotte chased her to the backyard, but Mary tagged the clubhouse boards right before her.

"You got a head start!" she said. They both laughed, knowing they really didn't care who won. Charlotte moved the wooden slab door and went inside. "We should get some hinges on that thing."

Mary nodded as she leafed through her notebook. "My dad said we could use the leftover wood from the new shed. I was thinking it'd make a good roof."

Charlotte agreed. Anything would be better than the old tarp, which sunk in the middle every time it rained.

After deciding how they would position the boards, they began moving the wood. They worked together, carrying one plank at a time. When the last piece was dropped onto the pile, they noticed the light getting dim. Charlotte looked up to see the sun disappear behind a dark cloud. "Is it supposed to rain?"

"My mom said there might be a thunderstorm," Mary replied.

Charlotte sulked. Normally, she loved thunderstorms, but right now she didn't want to go back inside. Working on the fort made it easier to pretend she was somewhere else far away.

They had just started removing the tarp when Mary felt a drop of water on her nose. A few drops landed on Charlotte's head. Charlotte groaned as she re-tied her end of the string. Reluctantly, they crawled back into the clubhouse. This was a safe place as long as the rainstorm didn't turn into a lightning storm.

"What should we do now?" Mary asked.

The rain was falling steadily. Charlotte looked out the window, which was once part of the old shed. "We can play cards until the rain stops."

Mary agreed and took the deck from a small chest. She dealt the cards while listening to the rain pattering on the roof. Even as the tarp began to sag, they continued to play, hoping they wouldn't hear thunder.

"Mary! Charlotte!" Mrs. Albright called from the back porch.

They looked at one another and sighed before Mary scooped up the cards. "I guess we'll have to play inside," she said. Charlotte wasn't interested in cards anymore, but she nodded anyway and followed her into the house.

"There isn't even lightning, Mom," Mary said when they walked through the door.

"I know, but they're calling for thunderstorms, and I'd rather you be safe than sorry."

The girls shared a look of disappointment at the familiar saying and carried themselves into the living room. Suddenly, a loud crack made them both jump. The rumble echoed overhead. They peeked over at Mrs. Albright who gave them a knowing glance. "Don't look so miserable. You can have just as much fun inside."

Charlotte was doubtful. She sank onto the couch next to Mary.

"Why don't you play a board game?" Mrs. Albright said.

"A board game?" Mary's answer was a mix of surprise and disdain. "I think I'd rather clean my room."

Mrs. Albright chuckled. "Now that you mention it, your room could use a good cleaning."

Mary frowned. "On second thought, a board game sounds great." She hopped up, pulled Charlotte off of the couch with her, and went downstairs. Charlotte let herself be led away to Mr. Albright's office, where the games were stored. Even though it wasn't as exciting as being outside, the office was a nice alternative. She'd heard her parents say Mr. Albright was one of the best lawyers in town and it sparked her curiosity of what exactly lawyers do.

Mary skimmed the bottom shelf of the closet while Charlotte got comfortable in the swivel chair. She took a few spins before pulling up to the desk. The office furniture was dark and heavy with a light layer of dust on the surface. Mr. Albright must not have needed to work from home lately.

The work area was kept fairly neat, with only a pile of papers set to the side and a few books lying around. Mary was fumbling with the Monopoly cards in the background so Charlotte grabbed a pen and a sticky note and wrote a memo for Mr. A to organize the game closet. She stuck it to one of the binders and spotted a gold pocket watch in the corner. *I thought only grandfathers had these. Mr. Albright must be older than I thought,* she reasoned.

This watch was heavier than her grandfather's though and the cover was spotless.

As she held it, she felt a slight hum through her fingertips. A faded inscription was etched on the back.

For a time where adventure awaits.

Shouldn't it say "when"? Flipping it open, she was surprised to see the secondhand circling rapidly. Even the hour hand was moving too fast. That would account for the vibration. Instead of ticking, the flying hands were buzzing.

She snapped it shut. *Didn't watches usually just stop when they were broken anyway?*

Mr. Albright probably wouldn't keep that for long.

She set it down and opened one of the thick books nearby. The words were hardly understandable and she was grateful they had never been on her vocabulary tests. As the book shut with a thump, a piece of paper fluttered to the ground. She scooped it up and saw it was a poorly scribbled note written on a strip of legal paper. Her eyes grew wide.

"Mary, I think I found something!"

Chapter Two

The Edge of the Woods

M ary, who was on the hunt for the missing Monopoly card, set the game down and joined Charlotte. Charlotte began reading the note in her hand.

I know you weren't fond of this neck of the woods, but I want the land kept in the family. As my last living relative, I'm leaving you the house and your rightful inheritance.

Mary shrugged. "That's just the note my dad's uncle left in his will," she said as she pointed to a thin folder marked, *The Last Will and Testament of Richard James Albright*. "It's about the house we looked at the other day."

"What was the inheritance?" Charlotte could hardly contain her excitement as she pulled the folder closer. She imagined a room full of treasure.

"What do you mean? The house *is* the inheritance, silly."

Charlotte gestured to the note again. "It says he's leaving him the house *and* his inheritance. Doesn't that mean there's more?"

"My dad only mentioned the property." She pointed to the watch on the side. "Maybe that's the inheritance. It doesn't work right but it could be an heirloom."

Charlotte wasn't convinced. "An old watch that doesn't work isn't an inheritance. Maybe it's something inside the house!"

"If it is, my parents will never find it," Mary said. "They wouldn't set foot in there again."

Charlotte barely heard her though. She was too busy looking through the papers in the folder. "I can hardly tell what they say," she admitted. "It's like this is in another language."

Mary walked back to the closet. "I don't think there's anything else to know. Help me find the last red card and we can play till the rain stops."

Charlotte was hoping for more than a game of Monopoly, but she figured Mary was right. She picked up the papers to straighten them out, but the last page kept drooping backward. Noticing the paperclip attached, she turned the pile over and saw a thick, brown sheet tucked underneath. It looked so strange that for a moment, she hesitated.

But only for a moment.

Carefully unfolding the parchment, she admired the beautiful illustrations and the unusually written script. Soon her mouth fell open. "A map!" she exclaimed. Unable to tear her eyes away, she traced the lines on the mysterious drawings with her fingertip.

Mary walked over, her eyebrows creased. "A map of what?"

"I don't know. It was attached to the will. I bet it's the treasure your uncle talked about!" Her eyes shone brightly.

"Inheritance," Mary corrected.

Charlotte ignored the comment. "Where did you say he lived again?"

"Parch Street."

"That's only a mile from here. We can find the treasure and your family will be rich!"

Mary pushed up her glasses. "We don't even know what the map is for. My dad said Uncle Richard was losing his mind, talking about magic or fairies or something. He might've thought *anything* was worth hiding:

old photos, his cat, a pile of rocks..." She threw up her hand in emphasis. "Besides, it looks like the map is torn in half. There isn't even an 'X' on it."

"Maybe the treasure is at the end of this line. Anyway, if he did hide his cat, we should probably go find it," she said with a smirk. Charlotte thought she saw the corners of Mary's mouth turn up. She gave Mary her best puppy-eyed look. This could be the perfect distraction from the new baby.

Mary chewed her bottom lip. "But shouldn't we let my dad find it? The map *was* left for him."

"It's not like we're going to keep what we find. Plus, your dad hardly has time to sleep, let alone hunt for an old man's treasure. Really, we're doing him a favor."

Mary knew there was no way to talk Charlotte out of it. She could be as stubborn as a mule when she set her mind to something. She also couldn't help but feel a little excited about where the map might lead. "I guess we can go if my parents say it's okay."

Charlotte clapped her hands excitedly and wiggled with glee.

"We should wait until Saturday though, so we have more time," Mary said.

That night before dinner Charlotte's parents were attempting to install the new car seat. Charlotte jumped in the front seat peering at them squished together in the back. They were both bent over trying to figure out where another clip should go. Neither of them realized they had company until Charlotte began talking. "I found a map today at Mary's house! Her uncle left it for them so that they could find a treasure! Can I go find it with Mary? Please!"

Her mom brushed the hair from her face and glanced up. "What Charlotte? What are you saying?"

Charlotte began again but then her dad pinched his finger and Mrs. Jenkins had to help put the clip in place. Charlotte tried to get her mom's attention again.

"So, can I go, Mom?"

"Where, honey?"

"With Mary to her uncle's house."

"Uhh, sure honey. Just be home before dinner."

Charlotte jumped out of the car excited to be able to go on a treasure hunt.

Since Tuesday was only a half-day, most of the classes were allowed to watch movies or play games. Mrs. Harding, however, was making her class catch up on missing assignments. Charlotte stared at the pile of missing work on her desk, which Mrs. Harding so readily provided. It made her feel like a caged bird with clipped wings. Even if she escaped, she wouldn't get far. Mary was the only one who hadn't missed a single assignment, so she was allowed to read or play on the computer.

Charlotte tried dutifully to focus. *Only a few more days,* she thought to herself. *Just a few days until I'm free.* She tried her best to concentrate, but her mind kept wandering to the map. She wanted so badly to find out where it would lead.

By ten o'clock, she was only halfway through her pile, and Mrs. Harding had to scold her repeatedly for daydreaming. Fortunately, the next few days would be end-of-the-year parties and field days, so Mrs. Harding would have to let them out.

The rest of the week flew by quickly and the busyness helped take the girls' minds off the map during school hours. In the afternoons, they would talk for hours about what they might find, and their imaginations would run wild. On Friday, Charlotte was so impatient, she was lucky she didn't have to sit still for long.

As the other kids were finishing cleaning out their desks, Charlotte sat, briskly bouncing her leg up and down. She'd already shoved all the contents of her desk into her backpack and finished her chore of wiping down the chalkboard. There was nothing left to do but wait. She watched the second-hand tick down until, finally, the last school bell rang.

Charlotte jumped from her chair so quickly, that it fell backward. She flinched when it crashed to the floor. Surprisingly, Mrs. Harding didn't look up. "Have a nice summer, Miss Jenkins," she said. "Be sure to pick up your chair before you leave." She glanced over with a trace of a grin before dismissing the other children.

"Sorry, Mrs. Harding! Th- thank you, Mrs. Harding." Charlotte smiled sheepishly as she righted the chair, grabbed her bag, and met Mary at the door. They'd agreed to meet in their fort after school to finish their plans. They were both talking excitedly on the way home and nearly fell out of the bus when it stopped.

Their parents had already given them permission to look around the property as long as they did not, under any circumstances, go near the house. Well, that's what Mary's parents had said at least. The girls had promised, thrilled to be able to go at all.

After dropping her book bag off at home and grabbing a snack and her overnight bag, Charlotte rode her bike as fast as she could to Mary's house. She'd be staying the night there so they could get an early start the next morning. Mary was already in the fort when Charlotte ducked inside. She turned her notebook for Charlotte to see.

"These are the directions my dad gave me. We can ride our bikes. That will give us more time to get there and back before dinner." They made a list of everything they'd need, including water bottles, a flashlight, and a compass Charlotte's dad had given her. After realizing how bulky their backpack would be, though, they decided the broken binoculars weren't essential. They packed Mary's backpack with the supplies and set everything by the front door. After eating dinner with Mary's family, they went to bed early hoping it would make the morning come more quickly.

But they could hardly sleep. Every time one of them shut their eyes, the other would think of something else to say. Finally, after being shushed by Mrs. Albright for the third time, they drifted off to sleep.

When the alarm went off at 7:00 a.m., Charlotte groaned and rolled over. Mary turned off the noise and reached for her glasses. She nudged Charlotte, who groaned again. Leaning over, she whispered, "It's time to go treasure hunting."

Charlotte opened her eyes wide. *It's finally here!* It didn't take long before she was fully awake. They hurried to get dressed and ate as much breakfast as they could sit still for. Afterward, they gathered their things, pulled on their hiking boots, and went out the front door. Uncle Richard's property was heavily wooded and the boots would help with the terrain. Suddenly, Charlotte turned and ran back into the house. When she came out again, the pocket watch was dangling from her hand. "Just in case," she said.

In no time, they were on their bikes, riding to Parch Street. The tread of the boots felt awkward on the pedals as they rode down the street but soon they hardly noticed. The morning was warm and breezy without a cloud in sight. Perfect weather for exploring.

Charlotte could hardly contain her excitement. She chatted with Mary happily, enjoying the sun on her back and the wind in her face. Lifting her arms off the handles to catch the breeze, she smiled. Her troubles at home seemed far away right now—just how she liked them.

Familiar houses passed by as they rode up and down the hills. When they swerved around the corner of Parch Street, Mary led the way to the cul-de-sac at the end of the street. She stopped in front of a long, dirt driveway lined with trees. Charlotte pulled up beside her. "Why'd you stop?"

Mary shrugged her shoulders. "I don't know," she replied. "I just have a weird feeling, like there is something down there." Charlotte glanced down the ordinary-looking driveway.

"I think you're right," she replied solemnly.

"You do?"

"Yes. It's called treasure!" Her eyes gleamed as she pushed her bike forward.

Mary laughed and shook her head, but she followed her friend down the long drive. The rain from last week had made the earth soggy, forcing them to dodge several mud puddles. When they reached the end, they dropped their bikes in the yard and looked around.

The house stood far back and was surrounded by low, overgrown shrubs. In some places, thick vines had pulled the siding from its place. Charlotte examined the layers of leaves and branches that coated the roof. She wondered how the house had become so run down.

"He spent the last year or so of his life in a nursing home and didn't hire anyone to take care of the house," Mary said, answering her thoughts.

Charlotte nodded. Despite its disarray, she couldn't pull her eyes away. Even after being battered by time and weather, the house had a certain appeal to it, as if it was made for something more. Before looking away, Charlotte noticed a small window in what seemed to be the attic. What was strange was the window looked brand new. While all the others were either cracked or missing panes this one was unbroken and spotless. Charlotte wondered if it was just a fluke. She turned to Mary who had already begun studying the map.

"According to this, we need to start at the edge of the woods by the oak tree." Mary held the map out for Charlotte to see. Charlotte let her thoughts of the house go as they made their way through the tangle of overgrown grass. When they reached the tree line, they were tingling with excitement.

"Are you ready?" Mary asked, a grin spread across her face.

"Ready!" Charlotte grabbed Mary's hand and together they stepped under the large oak tree.

Chapter Three

The Silver Knob

As they crossed into the forest, a strange sensation came over them. "I feel dizzy," Charlotte murmured, closing her eyes.

Mary held her head and sat on a nearby log.

"Maybe we should have eaten more for breakfast." The half of a bagel had seemed like a good idea at

the time. It would have been nearly impossible to sit any longer anyway.

Charlotte crouched down beside her. The ground felt safer than standing up. She nestled her face in her hands while her head spun. The sensation lasted a few moments, and it was a relief when it was over.

When they could stand again without toppling, the wide trail beckoned them along. The path was mostly dirt, with splotches of green grass spread throughout. Dandelions had sprouted everywhere, creating a speckled yellow landscape. Mary took some granola from her bag to nibble on. She hoped more food would keep her from feeling light-headed again.

Being in the forest so early was peaceful, and in a short while, they fell silent, watching the woods awaken. Squirrels were chattering close by, looking for their breakfast. Charlotte let a few crumbs fall from her hand and was soon dropping more than she had eaten. Mary warned her at first saying she'd be hungry later, but quickly changed her mind after seeing how close the squirrels were willing to come. After a minute, the animals had eaten more than the girls.

When the bag was empty, Mary stuffed it into her pocket. She was glad they'd brought lunch along too. The squirrels continued to scamper nearby until it was clear they'd receive nothing more. The girls had returned their attention to looking for clues. Even though it was unlikely there'd be an "X" on the ground, it'd be a shame to miss it if there was.

After a while, the sun grew hot on their backs, and their necks ached from looking up and down. It was getting hard not to feel discouraged. The woods stretched out in all directions, providing no help whatsoever. It was as if the forest never intended to end. To make matters worse, there hadn't been a single clue. They felt more and more miserable with every step.

When the sun shone directly above them, they decided to stop for lunch. Mary took out the picnic her mom had packed, and they ate hungrily. A stump in the ground made an uneven tabletop while they sat in a shady clearing. The leaves whistled in the wind offering a much-needed reprieve from the high-noon sun.

After polishing off her sandwich, Charlotte licked the peanut butter from her fingers. The water in the thermos was still cool and helped wash the food down. She glanced over at Mary. "Do you think we're getting close?"

Mary set her lunch aside and brushed away the crumbs. The map which had been put away was once again spread out before them. The line she thought they'd been following trailed off the edge of the paper. If there *was* another piece of the map, it would sure come in handy right now. She sat back on her heels and sighed heavily making her bangs flutter upward. "I don't know anymore."

A squirrel scurrying across the path stopped to pick up a piece of granola. Mary stared at the animal, puzzled. "I thought we were out of granola."

"We are," Charlotte replied looking up. "I must have dropped that piece earlier."

Mary buried her head in her hands. "Does that mean we've been going in circles?" Her words came out muffled. She peeked out between her fingers hoping for another explanation.

Charlotte opened her mouth to disagree but paused when she realized it made sense. The granola should be nowhere near them by now. Groaning, she flopped to her back. Mary did the same, and they were quiet for a while, watching the birds flutter from tree to tree.

Finally, Charlotte broke the silence. "We're wasting our time, aren't we?"

Mary shrugged and said, "Maybe. What if my uncle just thought he was a pirate?"

Charlotte laughed. Richard Albright *must* have been unusual to leave a treasure map in his will. But she hoped it wasn't all in his imagination.

The ground was cool on her back as she gently pulled the grass between her fingers. *Why hadn't he just put it in a bank and told Mr. Albright where to pick it up? Why go to so much trouble?* She considered all of the land he had. There were still a lot of woods left to explore. She leaned on her elbow as a thought occurred to her. "What about the path we saw a while back?"

Mary thought for a minute. "You mean that thin line of dirt?"

"It's something at least."

After a moment, Mary got up and shook the crumbs off. "Well, what are we waiting for?" She reached out to help Charlotte up, and they started again, confident they were going the right way this time. After all, it was the only other path they could see.

Hope filled their chatter as they quickly found the trail and followed it along, whacking away the underbrush with spindly sticks. It wasn't a hard trail to navigate, but it was long like the last one. They'd been walking for a while before Charlotte checked the time. "Ugh, my watch is dead. It still says eight o'clock."

Mary pulled out her phone and frowned. "Mine says 8:02 a.m. But everything else is working fine."

"Maybe it only *feels* like we've been walking for hours." Charlotte took the pocket watch from her bag and flicked it open. Surprisingly, the hour and minute hands had stopped spinning rapidly and the time read 12:32 p.m. The sun shining directly above made it clear it was close to accurate, if not spot-on.

Mary shook her head. "This doesn't make sense. Why is the broken watch working now and ours aren't?" She looked around, wondering where this trail was taking them. When she spotted her sandwich crust on a nearby stump, she growled in frustration. "Not again."

Seeing the bread a second later, Charlotte ran over and punted it like a football. It flung high in the air and landed in a nearby bush. She sat down on the stump with a huff. "Now we're stuck *and* we only have a defective watch to tell time." A nearby stick helped her vent her frustration as she broke it into little pieces.

Mary took off her glasses and rubbed her eyes. They'd been looking forward to this adventure for so long, it would be even more disappointing if it ended so quickly. While replacing her glasses, she heard a strange chirping sound. She looked up to see a bright red cardinal fly down to snatch up the sandwich crust. *At least we're making the animals happy today,* she thought. The bird flew off between two large oak trees with the bread hanging from its beak.

Suddenly, her face lit up. "I think we went the wrong way!"

Charlotte looked over, wondering if Mary had lost her mind.

"What I mean is, the line on the map keeps going left. Even though the trail starts to the left, it eventually turns right. So maybe we're not supposed to follow the trail at all."

The look on Charlotte's face was blank.

"I think we need to make our own path," Mary stated. Walking over to the dense brush, she examined the barrier. The bushes grew high overhead and spread out in all directions. Moving the branches aside without getting scratched by the tangled brush seemed to be impossible. She inhaled sharply and retreated as her finger oozed with blood from a particularly sharp barb. It was like the bushes had grown into a wall, intending to keep everyone out.

"What about over here?" Charlotte stood a little farther down where the thick brush offered a slight break. Before Mary could join her, she had already turned sideways, squeezing her way through. Even though it was only a few feet wide, the brambles pulling every which way made it a slow process. With only a few inches remaining, Charlotte tried to push free. Instead, her head jerked back causing her to yelp. She reached up to rub the sore spot. "I think I'm stuck."

Mary hastily stepped into the thorny bushes to help and soon regretted her carelessness. Her hands flew up to shield her face and she gritted her teeth against the painful grazes. When she made it to the other side, she rubbed her arms before carefully untangling her friend's hair. This was one of the few times she was glad her hair was sleek and straight. Even though the thorns still got caught, they were much easier to pull out.

Charlotte squirmed impatiently, making Mary prick her finger more than once. "Hold still!" she cried.

Charlotte simply huffed. She was willing to cut her hair off if it meant seeing what was in front of her. With her head pulled back, all she could see was that they were still in the forest.

After finally being freed from the web of thorns, she looked around excitedly. Apparently, the fact that they were still in the forest *was* all there was to see. Trees and shrubs grew closely together, making it difficult to look very far ahead. The only difference about this side of the "wall" was that it was more overgrown than the other.

A thread of a path ended a few feet from the bushes, but the forest had taken over the rest. There was no way they were going to stop now, so they decided to make a new path.

Leading the way, Mary did her best to walk in a straight line. With everything being so wild, however, this proved to be difficult. Broken tree limbs dangled from above and exposed roots jutted up to their knees, making it hard to navigate.

The brambles growing from the forest floor, though, proved to be the biggest challenge. These unruly bushes left little room to move around, and their scraggly arms pricked the girls' limbs as they passed by. The small amount of light filtering through the thick canopy made it difficult to dodge most of them.

The pair became so focused on protecting themselves, that they hardly noticed the trees beginning to part. Not until she saw grass at her feet did Mary bother to look up. She stopped abruptly, causing Charlotte to collide with her back.

"A little warning next-" But her sentence broke off as Charlotte gazed at the large expanse in front of them.

"A meadow," Mary almost whispered.

"In the middle of the forest?" Charlotte felt she had to whisper, too.

"Uncle Richard must've had more land than we thought." The view in front of them was a stark contrast to what they'd just come through. Instead of wild, dense overgrowth, there was a sea of white petals rippling like water in the gentle breeze. The flowers grew together so closely, that there was hardly an inch between them.

In the center of the enormous field stood a large tree. Eagerly, Mary checked the map and found it to be identical. "We found it!"

But Charlotte was already on her way. Suddenly, she froze, staring hard at the ground. With Mary now at her side, she held out her foot and gently took another step. Just as she suspected, the flowers parted magically around her. The girls looked at one another in disbelief.

Reaching down, Mary held her hand close to a blossom. It pressed itself against her. "It's as if they're alive- as alive as you and me."

"What is this place?" Charlotte asked. They carefully made their way to the tree, mesmerized by the flowers' movements.

Up ahead, the tree's thick, dark branches stretched upward, intertwining with themselves. What began as one solid trunk turned into three stalks, interweaving like a beautiful braid to the top. Branches covered with honey-colored leaves reached out from the center of the woven tree. It looked so majestic amid the white background, that they had to stop and catch their breath. Circling the tree slowly, they took in its beauty.

"Do you think this is the treasure?" Mary asked.

"A tree?"

"The land. It could be my dad's inheritance."

Charlotte scrunched up her face. She wasn't ready to accept plants over gold and jewels, no matter how amazing they were. "Remember there's still more to the map."

Recalling why they'd come in the first place, Charlotte urged Mary to look for clues. The flowers had stopped about six feet from the trunk in a perfect circle. She pushed the soil aside with her shoe, searching for signs below, but underneath the dirt was only more dirt.

Mary stepped further back, unsure what she should be looking for. It was hard to focus on finding clues when the surrounding scene begged to be admired. The tree's crowded leaves made it difficult to see much of anything anyway. In her mind, it wouldn't be so bad if this beautiful place ended up being the only treasure they found.

The breeze picked up, occasionally offering better glimpses of the braided trunk beneath the leaves. Other than its unusual shape, it seemed the same as any other tree. A squirrel skittered across a branch, holding an acorn in its mouth. He stopped and eyed her suspiciously as his tail twitched back and forth in warning. "Don't worry, that nut is all yours," she said with a laugh.

She ventured to the other side to give him some space. Charlotte was still inspecting the ground, making sure every inch was covered. Mary started at the bottom of the tree as she had before, and studied her way up. About halfway to the top, a glint of light caught her eye. *Is the sun reflecting off of some water?* The ground and flowers were all dry, however, as if it hadn't rained in weeks. *Strange, given the number of mud puddles we avoided on the way here.*

The sun was angled in such a way that made it difficult to look upward. Shielding her eyes, she changed her position to put the light at her back, doing her best to keep her eye on the spot in question. The glare reflected off of the trunk a second time. Now, with more determination she stayed in place and waited. Suddenly, she felt a pang of excitement. "Charlotte, come over here!"

Charlotte, who was now hunting around the base of the trunk for clues, joined her in the meadow.

"How far do you think you can climb?" Mary asked, looking up at the tree. She knew she wouldn't be able to go nearly as high as her friend.

Charlotte studied the tree strategizing the number of options she had for climbing. The only challenge was the distance to the first branch from the ground. "Give me a lift to the first branch and I think I can get pretty far. Why do you ask?"

"It looks like there might be something up there that we should check out."

Charlotte followed the line of sight to where Mary was pointing. The leaves remained motionless, revealing nothing unusual. Trusting Mary's judgment, she followed her back to the tree. The lowest branch was about seven feet from the ground. Mary crouched underneath it, letting Charlotte sit on her shoulders. The trunk was the perfect means of support.

Mary stood up unsteadily. "You're getting too heavy for this." She felt the weight even more when Charlotte put her feet on her shoulders and hoisted herself up. She rubbed her shoulders while calling out directions.

Even though the limbs were ideal for climbing, the bark was not. Charlotte did her best to climb quickly without slipping, firmly planting each foot before putting weight on it. After carefully wriggling over a few limbs, she scooted in close to the trunk. Other than the tree's smooth surface, however, nothing seemed out of place.

The trunk was far too wide to wrap her arms around, but she reached as far as she could, leaning to the right and then the left. She paid close attention to the feel of the grain. The slick surface made it easy to notice any irregularities.

It was the bark under her left hand that finally revealed the small nick. Tracing it with her fingertips, it proved to be a thin line curving downward. Holding tightly to the branches above her, she made her way around and finally sat in front of her discovery.

Her eyes grew wide when she saw a silver knob attached to a tiny door.

"You were right!"

"There's a clue?"

"There's a door!"

Mary wasn't sure she heard her right, but Charlotte was too excited to explain.

She gripped the knob, holding her breath in anticipation. Soon, sunlight flooded the open space, revealing a folded piece of paper lying inside. It looked oddly familiar.

"Charlotte, what do you see?" Mary asked impatiently.

Carefully unfolding the thick, brown parchment, Charlotte gasped. "It's the other half of the map!" She heard a squeal below.

"Bring it down and we'll put it together!"

Tucking it into her shirt pocket, she began the climb down. *What if there's more?* she thought. Quickly re-positioning herself, she stuck her hand back inside the doorway. The floor of the hideaway was smooth and empty.

The sides were more of the same but when she reached toward the ceiling, she found she couldn't touch the top. Stretching in as far as she could, her finger grazed something cold. A flash of worry crossed her mind and she recoiled hoping it wasn't anything that would bite.

Taking a minute to think, she decided to grab it anyway, figuring a creature would've either attacked her or run away by now. It was still there, but each time her finger brushed the object it would sway out of reach.

Slightly irritated, she sidled up against the trunk, stretching her arm farther than she thought possible. Her cheek was pressed tightly against the bark while she closed her eyes and waited for the perfect timing. As soon as it bumped against her fingers she grasped the end of the small, thin object and pulled.

Nothing happened.

She pulled harder.

Suddenly, she was thrown off balance as the piece released. She clung to the branch sideways, praying not to fall, and held the object firmly in her hand. Mary called up worriedly.

After steadying herself and calming her nerves, Charlotte glanced down. "It's a key. But I already opened the door." She looked at the object in confusion while Mary clapped her hands excitedly and told her to hurry down.

Charlotte scrambled from one branch to another with her discoveries. Now that she was on the first limb, the ground seemed strangely far away. Looking around her, she gasped. Everything was being raised farther and farther into the air. The tree was growing right underneath her feet!

She crouched down, wrapping her arms around the trunk. Mary, who was now running around frantically, grew more and more distant. The tree only grew faster, causing the wind to whistle past like a boiling teapot. She plastered herself against the limb, squeezing her eyes shut and holding on with every bit of her strength. A few moments passed before it finally slowed and eventually stopped.

Charlotte's face stayed pressed against the cool bark. Leaves from the branch above swept along her back, enticing her to stir. Even though she knew it was no longer moving, she couldn't bring herself to loosen her grip.

After a long while, she opened one eye. Her stomach turned. *I must be at least fifty feet from the ground!* She heard Mary calling but was still too stunned to speak. Birds flew by, making the height seem like no trouble at all. One perched on a branch across from her, eyeing her suspiciously. She figured she probably looked pretty odd as the strange new lump on the tree.

Eventually, her head stopped reeling enough to sit up. The bird flew off at the sudden movement. As she watched it in the distance, she tried to decide what to do. Her thoughts felt jumbled. *Breathe, Charlotte. You can do this.*

The branch holding her didn't feel very sturdy, but she felt she was out of options. It was too high up to climb down safely and the other branches seemed so far away.

Mary called out again. "I'm alright," Charlotte responded, trying to keep the quiver from her voice. Taking another deep breath, she scanned her surroundings. The large bough with the tiny door seemed to be the best bet. If taking the key made the tree grow, maybe putting it back would make it shrink again. It was worth a try.

Even after making a plan though, her body refused to move. Heights had never been a problem before, but the thought of climbing around while this high up was anything but comforting. Digging into the soft bark and gritting her teeth, she forced her legs to stand up. Whatever was in reach helped steady her as she gradually moved through the limbs, determined not to look down.

She scaled two more branches and had to lean against the trunk to grab the third. Fortunately, her hands had a firm grasp before her foot slipped from the smooth surface, leaving her dangling in mid-air. Her heart leaped into her throat as she clung desperately to the branch above. Her toe was barely able to graze the spot where she'd been standing. It'd be impossible to get back now.

A limb that was closer and a little higher than her waist offered some hope. It was no bigger than her leg, but it would have to do. Her arms were already burning and wouldn't hold out much longer. Kicking against the trunk, her body swung sideways. After gaining enough momentum, her foot caught the bough easily enough, helping pull her over. When she sat firmly atop, she waited until her hands stopped trembling. She decided at that moment she never wanted to climb a tree again.

After several shaky breaths, she wiped her sweaty palms down her jean shorts. It didn't help. *This is just like the tree in my backyard,* she told herself. *A tree I've climbed a hundred times before. It's a regular, very normal tree. A normal tree that somehow grows in an instant.* Then, ignoring every reason not to, she continued the climb as if she wasn't fifty feet in the air.

When she finally rested on the sturdy branch, a great sigh of relief came out involuntarily. Beads of sweat clung to her forehead and her throat was too dry to swallow. She'd be content to stay there for the rest of her life if it meant never having to climb another inch.

The air felt cooler now and a light fog had crept in, making it impossible to see her friend. She called down but didn't hear a response. She hoped Mary had gone for help. As she scooted closer to the trunk, she suddenly stopped. The height seemed to be playing tricks with her eyes. Instead of a tiny silver knob, an ornate golden handle was now attached to a very large door. *Isn't this the same branch I was on before?* She looked all around her. *But where did this come from?* It was as though the door had grown along with the tree.

This day could *not* get any stranger.

Dumbfounded, she stared at the door as if it might change again. But it simply stared back as though it had been there all along. The long handle gleamed in the sunlight, inviting her in, but her adventurous side had waned from the terrifying climb up. All she wanted was for the tree to shrink again so she could go home. *So much for wanting an adventure,* she thought.

Hesitatingly, she began to lean forward but caught herself. There could be anything behind this door. *What if it was some kind of trap? What if it only made things worse? Whoever had set this up clearly didn't want anyone to find it. On the other hand, what else am I going to do? Climb down?*

Not a chance.

Choosing the less troubling of the two, she sucked in her breath and once again reached for the handle.

Chapter Four

The Fox and His Den

Mary paced back and forth underneath the now gargantuan tree. The thumbnail she'd been nervously chewing on now had nothing left. The place where Charlotte had been sitting was long out of sight. At least Charlotte had called down to her to let her know she was alright. Now she just had to find a way to get her down.

The items they'd brought with them were useless for this sort of thing. Water bottles, money, a pocket knife... nothing that could help now.

"Why didn't we *plan* to be stuck in a tree?" Even as she said it, she knew the thought was ridiculous. Charlotte would've laughed if she'd heard her.

Sitting back on her heels, her head began to throb. All this worry was starting to cause a headache. Suddenly, she remembered the cell phone she had brought for emergencies. She chided herself for not thinking of it sooner. Mr. Albright's number was at the top of the list. Hopefully, he wasn't in a meeting. After tapping the screen, the phone tried to dial. After a long period of silence, it still refused to connect.

No signal. Not one bar.

The phone made a clunking sound as it fell to the bottom of the bag. She thought to run for help, but the map was still in Charlotte's pocket. It would be tricky trying to find the way back even *with* the map, let alone without it. She was running out of options.

A strange fog had settled around the tree hiding her friend from view. The tree had grown so tall, that she wasn't even sure where it ended. The thought of how worried Charlotte must be made her take a shaky breath.

"I'll just have to rescue her myself."

With even the lowest branches now high in the air, it was hard to find a good place to begin. Luckily, around the other side, a large knot stuck out from the otherwise smooth trunk. It was a few feet from the ground and offered the perfect foothold.

Getting a good grip, she hoisted herself up. Even if there was nowhere to go from there, she had to at least try. As the bump held her weight, however, something strange began to happen. The knot slowly started to turn. Her foot slid off and she tumbled to the ground. "What on earth..?"

Scrambling to her feet, she brushed the dirt from her jeans and examined the knot more closely. There was nothing unusual about it other than it was the only one. As she grappled with it, it turned reluctantly in her hand.

On a hunch, she gave it a hard tug causing a section of the tree to inch forward. Stepping back, she saw the outline of a door. She gasped and pulled harder on the knot, opening it just enough to squeeze her fingers through the crack. With both hands now gripping the opening, she leaned backward using her full weight as leverage. The bottom of the door made a rough grinding sound as it was dragged along the ground. Finally, it opened wide enough for her to fit through.

After staring in wonder at the open doorway, she timidly poked her head inside. A tall spiral staircase rose upward, neatly carved around the sides of the tree. She stared at the steps in amazement. There appeared to be no end in sight. Even still, it was relieving to find a way up that didn't involve scaling the outside of the tree. Praying this way would lead to Charlotte, she took the first step.

* * *

Charlotte pressed the handle and pushed the door inward. It creaked forward, eventually revealing a large room within. She blinked several times. Maybe the height *was* making her imagine things. But then again, here she was fifty feet in the air. And *that* was definitely real.

There was no chance of returning the key now, but at least she'd be surrounded by walls. She was still gazing in wonder as she crawled inside. The ceiling stretched high above her making it easy to stand up. The room was breathtaking. Arches were carved into the vaulted ceiling while several stained-glass windows flooded the space with light.

Charlotte traced her fingers over the door frame. The carvings seemed to be telling a story, one she couldn't yet understand. In the center of the room, a tired-looking armchair faced an unlit fireplace.

"A fireplace in a tree? This can't possibly be real." There was, however, a small bundle of wood stacked against the wall.

A black and white photograph of a man and a fox stood framed on the mantel. The fox appeared to be dressed in an old-fashioned suit. Even so, she had no idea a fox could be a pet, but she decided to ask for one when she got home.

Crossing the dusty rag rug, she peered at the built-in bookcase. The shelves were lined with small trinkets and what appeared to be ancient books. Next to this, a small cabinet jutted out of the wall. Inside, a thin yellow jar marked, "Stunning Powder," sat on the top shelf. The lower shelf held a tall, unlabeled bottle of clear liquid.

Charlotte's mouth suddenly felt parched. She took the unmarked bottle from its place and examined the liquid. It looked just like water. The cork took a little twisting to remove but finally popped out. The smell of grape wafted toward her. She smiled. Grape was her favorite. She knew it wasn't a good idea to drink strange things, but her mouth felt as dry as sandpaper and the bottle smelled *so* good. *A little sip shouldn't hurt,* she thought. Carefully, she put the bottle to her lips.

Once the cool liquid touched her tongue she couldn't resist gulping down the refreshing drink. The fluid was not only delicious but instantly quenched her thirst. She set what was left of the bottle on the bookcase and walked over to the cluttered desk. Mary's uncle clearly wasn't as organized as her father. A jumble of papers lay scattered across the desk's surface. *What could Mary's uncle have been doing out here? Wasn't he too old for tree forts?* Suddenly, a loud thud came from below.

Then another, *THUD.*

"Charlotte? Charlotte, are you there?"

"Mary?! How did you get under the floor?"

"I climbed the stairs. There's a door but it's stuck."

Charlotte pushed back the dusty rug to uncover a trap door below. A semi-round crevice had been cut out to form a handle. She gripped the opening and pulled, but the door wouldn't budge. It was either stuck or locked. The small keyhole near the divot gave her an idea. *Maybe this is what the mysterious key is for.* Taking the item from her pocket, she inserted it into the hole and turned. *Click.* She tried pulling the door up again and was relieved to see Mary's worried face looking up at her.

Mary threw her arms around her neck, nearly pulling her over. "Am I glad to see you! And all in one piece!"

"Me too! And I'm really glad to see there's another way down." Charlotte laughed as she helped Mary into the room. She closed the door while Mary knelt on the floor catching her breath.

"What is this place?"

"Apparently, it grew with the tree," Charlotte replied.

"Do you think my uncle knew about it?"

"I think it's why the map led us here. Is that him up there?" Charlotte pointed to the photograph on the mantel. The picture was old but Mary could see the resemblance to some of her dad's old photos. She remembered one she liked in particular of her dad smiling while Uncle Richard propped him on his shoulders. "It does look like him. He looks even younger than in my dad's photos though. I didn't know he had a fox."

"I'm going to get one when we get back," Charlotte replied confidently. "But now we need to find the next clue." Mary set the picture back on the shelf. She didn't understand how her great-uncle had a magical tree in his backyard, or why her dad never mentioned it. Maybe he never knew.

She wandered around the room leaving Charlotte to rummage through the desk. The tree fort was not what she would have expected. Rather than rough and unfinished, the walls were smooth with meticulous carvings. The comfortable furnishings made her feel at ease and she took her time looking through the contents on the bookshelf.

Charlotte glanced up. "There's some grape juice there if you want it."

Mary picked up the bottle. "Clear grape juice? Where did it come from?"

"The cabinet." She nodded her head toward the wall.

Mary took off the cork and smelled the contents. "Are you sure it's grape juice? It smells like cherry to me."

Charlotte shrugged.

Mary didn't like the thought of drinking something they'd just found. Charlotte didn't mind things like that though and she seemed to be doing alright. She tried a sip. It tasted pretty good. She decided to drink only enough to make her feel better.

Meanwhile, Charlotte sifted through another stack of papers on the desk. They felt so fragile in her calloused hands. Each page had a unique symbol on it with a small etching of words underneath.

"Mary, look at this." She held up a drawing of an ornate crown. The crown had both large and small jewels encased around the rim.

"It's beautiful."

Charlotte looked closely at the cramped words scribbled next to the illustration. All she could make out was the number four. "I wonder if this is the treasure."

"Nothing seems impossible anymore," Mary admitted, gesturing to the room which appeared out of thin air. She wondered about their discoveries while absently running her finger along the desk. It left a line where it had traveled. She found an old piece of cloth, lifted the papers, and wiped the desk off. Then she moved on to other areas of the room.

Charlotte knew something was on Mary's mind when she went into cleaning mode. Her room was always immaculate the day before a test. Discovering a magical tree fort in her uncle's backyard was definitely a lot to think about. Mary picked up the rug and stood in the doorway shaking it out.

With the door open, a cool breeze came through, making the girls shiver. Dark clouds had gathered in the distance and the wind picked up. Mary closed the door tightly and quickly shut the open window. "I think a storm's coming in." The rug was laid down again and the dust rag hung in the corner.

The chilly air made the fireplace seem even more inviting. "It would be nice to start a fire right now," she said and sat back in the chair to rest. Before Charlotte could open her mouth to object, the fireplace roared to life. Mary sat up in disbelief.

"How did you do that?!" Charlotte asked.

"I didn't!"

Both girls walked over to the fire. The heat warmed their hands and faces. "Maybe it's set on a timer," Mary suggested. Charlotte looked skeptical but she couldn't think of another explanation.

Suddenly, a small rustling sound came from beneath the trap door. Mary looked at Charlotte and could tell she was equally alarmed. "What is that?" She felt as though she'd been caught doing something she shouldn't.

"Maybe my brothers followed us here. They're always trying to mess with us." Even as she said it though, Charlotte knew that was unlikely. The noise came again. She worked up her nerve and stammered, "Who... who's down there?"

"Who's down *here*?" Came an annoyed response. "I demand to know who's up *there*!"

Chapter Five

A Startling Revelation

Charlotte moved closer to the trap door, relieved to know she had re-locked it. "Whoever you are...just go away," she shouted, a little louder than she meant to. The voice became indignant.

"I most certainly will *not* go away! You, my dear, are trespassing so I suggest *you* go away. Immediately!"

"Trespassing?" Mary asked. "We are not trespassing! This is my parents' land and we have every right to be here." Even as she said it though, she wasn't completely sure if it was true. The girls heard a key fit into the lock. *Click.* Charlotte stepped back taking hold of Mary's arm.

"If he seems dangerous, be ready to run."

"Where would we run?" Mary asked. "Onto a limb?" Charlotte's eyebrows knit together in worry. Mary was right. If they got into trouble there would be nowhere to go. They backed up against the wall, putting as much distance as they could between themselves and the "intruder."

The trap door flung back, banging loudly on the floor. Mary squeezed her eyes shut not wanting to look. Surprisingly, an orange paw poked up from below.

Two furry ears appeared, followed by a narrow head and a long snout. "A fox!" Charlotte screamed. She quickly looked for something to defend herself. Mary opened her eyes when she heard the scream and was now screaming herself.

The fox cocked his head to the side, seeming genuinely amused. "Now surely you have both seen a fox before," he said matter-of-factly. Charlotte's mouth dropped open.

She stood frozen, clutching a broom above her head. Mary slumped against the wall.

After a minute Charlotte regained her bearings and slowly lowered the broom. "You can talk?" Each word seemed to catch in her throat. The fox climbed into the room and casually closed the door behind him. He now stood on his hind legs gazing over at the two.

"Of course, I can talk. I'm not a barbarian," he said with a chuckle. "I do remember my master having a similar reaction the first time we met. You must be from similar worlds." He shrugged this observation off, becoming more serious. "Now, tell me who you are and why you've come here. And how in Ilyor did you find this enchanted tree?"

Mary was slowly pulling herself from the wall. "The picture. Who is your master?" she asked softly, as if still in a dream-like state. The fox looked over, studying her.

Then with a lofty air, he said, "My master is Sir Richard Collins of Lexington." A concerned look passed over his face. "Although I haven't seen him in a while, I'm sure he will return soon, so you better start explaining yourselves." He finished by shaking his paw at the girls. Mary and Charlotte looked at one another worriedly.

"Um," Mary started. " Sir, uh, fox."

"My name is Humberly," he interrupted with a small bow before noticing the papers Charlotte had disturbed. Mary tried again.

"Sir Humberly..."

"Not sir," the fox interrupted again holding up a paw, "just Humberly. I am not a nobleman, simply a servant."

"Oh, I'm sorry." Mary started fidgeting with her nails.

Charlotte could tell she was losing her nerve.

"Look, Humbertly," Charlotte started. Humberly cast an annoyed glance her way. "Sorry. Humber-*ly*. Your master is not coming back." The fox stopped sorting papers and looked at her.

"And how would you know this?"

"Because, Richard Collins..."

"Sir Richard Collins," Humberly retorted.

"Excuse me. *Sir* Richard Collins, is Mary's great-uncle. And, well... he's dead."

Mary swatted Charlotte's arm. Charlotte glanced back sheepishly. She really needed to practice giving bad news more gently. But honestly, she was only ten. How much more practice could she have? Humberly dropped his gaze and stood staring at the floor. "It can't be." The papers slid from his hands as he sank into the desk chair. "When did this happen?" Mary took a small step forward.

"About two weeks ago. He was in the hospital for a while and then went into a nursing home. He passed away in his sleep." Mary hoped this last part would bring the fox some comfort. She knew it had made her feel better when her dad broke the news. She hadn't known her great uncle very well but she couldn't stand the thought of him being in pain. Humberly looked up helplessly.

"Did he leave anything behind?"

"Just his house. And this torn map," Charlotte offered.

"So, this is why you're here," Humberly said as he motioned to the map. "He led you to me."

Mary thought she saw a glimmer of hope in the fox's sad eyes. Humberly took the map in his hands. Charlotte removed the other half from her pocket and laid it on the desk in front of him.

"I'm Charlotte by the way." Humberly gave a small nod before piecing the map together. He gazed at it thoughtfully as Mary peered over his shoulder. In all the commotion, she had yet to see the other half. After a few minutes, Charlotte couldn't wait any longer. "Do you know where it leads?" Humberly took his time answering.

"The better question would be, 'do you know what it leads to?'"

"What do you mean?"

"This is no ordinary map. This map leads to a treasure fit for kings and queens. A treasure which can save Ilyor." Charlotte's eyes grew wide at the mention of treasure.

"I knew your uncle didn't bury a rock!"

Humberly looked puzzled.

"But what's Ilyor?" she asked, getting back on topic.

"And why does it need to be saved?" Mary added.

Humberly blinked at the sudden shifts in conversation before he began.

"Ilyor is the kingdom you're in now. It's where Sir Richard really belonged. As to why Ilyor needs saving, well, that will take longer to explain." Getting comfortable, he shifted in the chair and motioned for the girls to do the same. After they seated themselves on the rug, he began.

"You see, a long line of royalty reigned peacefully over Ilyor for many generations. The land and all who were in it prospered greatly under their rule, and many settled here because of it. Even though the king and queen were young at the time, they followed the path of their ancestors, devoting themselves to Ilyor's success.

"After a while, the queen bore a son and the kingdom rejoiced. As he grew, however, it became obvious there was something peculiar about him.

When others were learning the ways of light, he was fascinated by darkness. He often urged his parents to war against neighboring kingdoms, even allies, simply to gain power. He saw his parents' humanity as a weakness, and rather than help the people of Ilyor, he desired to control them.

"The king and queen argued tirelessly with their son, hoping he would see the error of his ways, but it was no use. The son's heart was filled with wickedness and he only continued to incite treachery and deceit. Fearing his eventual rule, his parents took vast measures to protect the kingdom. Consequently, before his 25th birthday, they had their only son exiled from the land and appointed their nephew to inherit the throne. This, of course, devastated them but had become the only solution.

"After the king and queen's passing, the nephew indeed became king and ruled as his aunt and uncle intended. He did right by the people and established himself as a just and fair ruler.

"However, after years of peace and safety, he became too comfortable and began taking Ilyor's welfare for granted. Rather than continuing to strengthen its military, he relied completely on the Meir and the crown's power for protection. While the Meir are very powerful, they are connected to the one who wears the crown. If they are not summoned by such, they can do very little.

"Unfortunately, this left Ilyor vulnerable and eventually, the attack came, as many knew it would. Upon hearing of his parents' death, the wicked son waited for the right moment before leading a large army to invade the kingdom. All of Ilyor fought against them but were ill-prepared and Ilyor was overcome. The son had the nephew killed and took possession of the land. His royal line has succumbed to the darkness ever since."

Humberly paused as if reflecting upon his own words before continuing. "The King wields the darkness to take control over more and more territory. There are many dark parts of the kingdom now and their realm grows every year. The only safe regions are the few protected by the Meir-and they can only do so much."

"What are the Meir?" Mary interjected.

"The Meir are beautiful spheres of color which represent all that is untainted in the world. They harness the power of light and can only be commanded by those who wear the crown. Fortunately, as one of their precautions, the king and queen put a powerful enchantment on the crown's gems ensuring only those uncorrupted can summon the Meir. However, without a righteous king or queen to rule, the Meir do not have the power to do what is needed. They can perform only minimal magic until an honorable leader unleashes their full potential.

"Sadly, the nephew was captured before calling on the Meir, leaving them powerless to defend the kingdom. Now they lie in wait until a rightful heir reclaims the throne and takes back what was lost." Humberly hesitated as realization dawned on him and looked knowingly at Mary. The girls had been sitting with their backs to the fire, mesmerized by the tale.

Mary didn't notice his eyes on her until Charlotte asked abruptly, "What will happen now?"

As usual, he took a moment to answer. "Well, I suppose that depends on you."

"Me?"

"No, not you, dear. Your friend here, Mary." Mary's eyes grew wide.

"Why me?"

"Because you are the next royal heir."

Chapter Six

Daring Decisions

Mary's jaw dropped. Slowly, she began to shake her head. "No, that can't be right. I am *not* royalty."

"You said Sir Richard Collins was your uncle, correct?"

"Well, yes, my great uncle... but what does that have to do with...?" she trailed off as he continued.

"Sir Richard Collins was the great-grandson of the king and queen's nephew. This put him directly in line for the throne. But now that he has passed away, you have become the next available heir." Mary and Charlotte sat speechless for a few moments. Then Mary glanced at Charlotte and her face broke into a grin. She covered her mouth, trying to stifle a giggle.

"I'm sorry, Humberly, but I really think you're mistaken." By the stern look on his face, the girls could tell he was not amused.

"I am certainly *not* mistaken. And it can easily be proved."

Mary quickly sobered. She watched as he reached into a hidden nook in the wall. "The rightful heir will be entitled to a crown. A crown with four of the most valuable gems in the land mounted on its brim."

He pulled a velvety black bag from the niche while he spoke. "As I said before, the gems were enchanted by the king and queen so that no one unworthy could control the Meir. Knowing this, and to prevent a rightful heir from taking his place, the evil son had the gems removed. And since they were too powerful to be destroyed, hid them throughout the land.

"But there is hope. Believing he would eventually learn to harness their power, a map was created to document their locations. Thankfully, there has yet to be an enchantment strong enough to surpass the first. Thus, neither the son nor his descendants had the necessary means to retrieve the crown, lest they be overcome by its power. Although the current king may still be foolish enough to try.

"Many others, both worthy and unworthy, have tried and failed. It became clear that without the map, the crown and its gems would remain lost. Therefore, your uncle and I took desperate measures. Being an excellent tailor, I went to work in the palace. It took some time, but after a year or so I finally gained the other servants' trust and learned where the map was being held.

"Little did I know, *that* would turn out to be the easy part. Sneaking into the king's chambers would prove far more difficult. The servants were either fiercely loyal or under some sort of spell, so I needed to enter the chambers without notice. This was challenging as they were constantly tidying and replenishing at the king's every whim.

"With so much activity, I often had to wait until the entire palace was distracted by some elaborate celebration. Thankfully, I was excused from these things, as the clothing was always finished long before they began. Even still, it took me a full year to trace the map in its entirety. When I finally had it replicated in full, I left the castle in the dead of night and returned here.

"I received word from one of the chambermaids, that the king was outraged when I did not return. Of course, no servant is allowed to leave the palace unless ordered to do so. If he catches me now, he will surely have me thrown in the dungeon." The girls shuddered at the thought of being kept in a dungeon. "I don't believe anyone is aware of what I've done, but your uncle and I decided to tear the map in half as an added precaution. We were able to secure one of the gems before he left, which will confirm what I am saying is true."

"But how will a gem prove anything?" Charlotte asked. Humberly opened the black bag and out slid the most beautiful stone the girls had ever seen. The deep ruby was the size of a silver dollar and sparkled in the light of the fire. Mary gasped. Everything in her was drawn to this jewel. As she reached out, it began to glow, which only captivated her more.

Finally, she held it in her hand, unable to look away. The stone grew warm and shone brilliantly throughout the cottage. Humberly beamed at Charlotte but she could only gaze in wonder at how Mary and the gem seemed to connect.

With Mary still drawn in, he quickly slipped it from her hand and Mary came back to reality. She released a deep breath as though she'd been holding it the entire time. "Have you ever seen anything so beautiful?" she finally whispered.

Humberly smiled. "Now you have proof you are meant to rule." Mary blushed, still unable to fully grasp the idea of being royalty.

"But how do we know that won't happen to anyone who holds that gem?" Charlotte asked.

"Simple," he said, moving far enough away from Mary before taking it out again. He opened Charlotte's palm and laid the stone inside.

Nothing.

The gem sat as lifelessly as it had in Humberly's paw.

"Point taken."

After reclaiming the jewel, he turned toward Mary and continued.

"Your uncle's desire was for his lineage to be restored to the throne. We secured the first gem before he returned to his world. When he left to 'tie up some loose ends,' we each kept a piece of the map and planned to journey to the next location when he returned. I kept my half in the enchanted tree and he took his half with him. Only, he never did return. And now I suppose he never will."

Mary felt sorry Humberly had lost someone so dear to him. She couldn't imagine losing someone she was close to. Then a thought occurred to her. "Wait. Why does the royal line skip to me and not my dad?"

Humberly let out a long sigh. "It wouldn't, if your father were willing to take his place. As you know, your uncle had no children of his own. He tried very hard to convince his only nephew, your father, of the reality of Ilyor. He, however, refused to believe and turned down every invitation, accusing your uncle of being a fool. He stopped visiting him years ago."

Now Mary understood why she hardly saw her uncle. She also knew why her dad refused to believe in this magical world. Even though he was an intelligent and kind man, he did not believe in what he thought were fanciful stories. He could be very argumentative when he disagreed with someone, which in turn made him a very good lawyer.

Suddenly, Mary lit up. "What about my sister? She would be part of the royal lineage too."

"You have a sister? Would she be willing to take the throne?"

Mary was about to say "yes" when Charlotte snickered, causing her to rethink the idea. Both girls enjoyed Katherine's spontaneity and that she was always up for a good time, but when it came to being responsible for others, it didn't exactly come naturally.

That had become obvious a few years ago when Katherine was supposed to watch Mary. About an hour after their parents had left, she decided she was bored and went to meet her friends instead. Sometimes Mary felt she acted older than Katherine did.

"Probably not," Mary answered honestly.

Humberly nodded. "Then it is up to us. We must find the rest of the gems so you can redeem Ilyor."

Mary was thoughtful for a few moments. "So, I'm the only one in Ilyor who can restore the kingdom?"

"That is correct," Humberly replied coolly.

"And if I don't, Ilyor will continue to be ruled by darkness?"

"Right again. I'm sure it will eventually be overrun completely."

Charlotte watched the color drain from Mary's face. "Why don't you sit down for a while?" She took Mary's arm and led her to the armchair.

"I can't be responsible for an entire kingdom," Mary said with a moan. "I'm only ten!" She rested her head back in the chair. "I think I'm gonna be sick."

"Don't worry," Humberly replied calmly. "It's in your blood. It will all come naturally."

Mary was not reassured.

"We just have to take it one step at a time," Charlotte said encouragingly. "Right now, all we have to do is search for treasure. Doesn't that sound exciting?" Mary smiled weakly.

"I certainly wouldn't describe this journey as exciting," Humberly interjected. "This map will lead us through very dark parts of the kingdom. The word 'dangerous' better fits the description." Charlotte glared at Humberly, who returned her look with a small shrug and continued about his business.

She turned back to Mary. "Listen, whatever you go through, I will be right beside you. And if anything is too scary, we'll turn around and go back. OK?" Mary thought for a minute. She looked over at Humberly.

"Is it really going to be dangerous?" she asked. Humberly was busily going through drawers and cabinets.

"Too dangerous not to be thoroughly prepared," he replied.

Charlotte skirted over the remark. "That doesn't sound too bad," she said cheerfully.

Mary was doubtful. Nonetheless, she knew she couldn't say "no" to something so important. "Okay. I'll go. But let's start tomorrow since it's getting late. I'm sure it will be dinner time soon." The thought of being home around the dinner table again helped lift her spirits. Maybe she'd even be able to convince Katherine or her dad to come back instead.

Charlotte looked out the window. It did seem to be getting late. She glanced down at her broken watch. The second hand had moved slightly but nothing more.

"What time is it, Humberly? My watch is broken."

Humberly glanced at his pocket watch. "4:30."

"We have to get back for dinner," Mary announced. "But Charlotte and I will come first thing after church tomorrow." *Or someone will come at least.*

Humberly looked blankly at Mary for a few seconds. "Oh, yes. I forgot. Your watch isn't broken, and there's no need to return home so soon. Time passes in your world very slowly once you cross Ilyor's threshold. You could spend days here and you would have only missed an hour or two in your time." Humberly continued to put things into a satchel as Mary and Charlotte gazed at him in disbelief.

"So, you're saying we could stay here for a month and we would still be back before anyone realized we were gone?" Mary asked. Her shoulders sank with disappointment.

"Oh yes, and much longer than that I'm sure. Sir Richard frequently stayed for months at a time. He kept one watch for this world and another for his. But we will wait until morning as you suggested. We have many more supplies to get first."

At the mention of the two watches, Charlotte pulled the pocket watch from her jeans. "Is this the watch you mean?"

Humberly took it from her hand. "I gave this to him as a gift when our adventures first began." He smoothed over the inscription on the front. "That was years ago now."

"If it's special to you, I'm sure my dad would want you to keep it," Mary said. "Even though the gears are acting up."

Humberly flipped open the cover. "It seems to be working just fine. This watch will run for ages if you take care of it. But no, he would want it kept in the family." He handed it over to Mary.

She flipped it open and sure enough, it read 4:30. "But it was spinning before and only stopped a few hours ago."

"It was always working properly. Our time simply moves at a much faster pace than yours."

"Now, about your clothing." Humberly walked over to the girls, shaking his head. "This surely won't do. We will have to make you more presentable. You certainly won't blend in wearing these scraps."

Charlotte's eyes widened at the insult. "This shirt was a present from my mom!"

Humberly leaned in and examined the bejeweled heart, not bothering to hide his disdain. "These gems are fake. I'm sorry you received such a poor gift."

Charlotte's mouth hung open, but he paid no attention and simply moved toward the desk to open a drawer filled with stones. "I'll take two of these to purchase more supplies. We can't have you seen looking like that."

Mary stepped past the now glaring Charlotte. "How will you buy supplies with a couple of rocks?"

The fox's eyebrows went up. "Rocks?" Now it was Humberly's turn to be offended. "A rock is something used to scrape mud off of your boot.

These, my dears, are gems. Highly valuable, precious, uncut gems. And they are the currency of Ilyor."

He slipped the stones into a pouch before turning on his heel. "I'll make a quick list of the supplies we still need. Your uncle has plenty of stunning powder here and there should still be a bottle of vanishing serum as well." He nodded toward the cabinet the girls had explored earlier.

A sudden thought occurred to Charlotte and she stiffened. "You mean in that small cabinet by the window?"

"That's the one," Humberly replied. Charlotte quickly pulled Mary aside. Mary chuckled at her sudden loss of balance but stopped when she saw the seriousness of her friend's face.

"I think we may have drunk one of the supplies."

Mary's eyes grew wide. "You mean the water?"

"Yes, only now I don't think it was water."

"What if it was poisonous?" Mary held her hands to her throat. "We better tell Humberly before it's too late."

Chapter Seven

An Unusual Problem

Charlotte grimaced and glanced over at Humberly. Mary poked her in the ribs which she repaid with a scowl. *Why do I always have to break the bad news?*

"Umm, Humberly?" Her voice came out hoarse.

"Hmm?" He barely replied, too preoccupied with his list. Charlotte forced herself to continue.

"Is the vanishing serum a clear liquid?"

"Mm-hmm."

"Clear...like water? And smells good?"

"Yes, dear. It smells like whatever flavor you most enjoy."

That's why it smelled differently to Mary than it did to me, Charlotte thought, momentarily off track. She refocused her thoughts.

"So it would make sense if someone drank some when they found it because they were really thirsty?"

"I suppose." Humberly nodded. Suddenly, he looked up. "Wait! You don't mean... did you actually drink some?!"

Charlotte shifted uncomfortably. "Well, not exactly. We sort of drank it... *all*."

"You did what?" Humberly almost shouted. He held his hand to his head, steadying himself. "If it were anything else, you could be dead!"

"We know. We're sorry. We were just really thirsty after climbing all of those stairs, and being shot into the air and..." Mary trailed off.

"Fine, fine," Humberly said, trying to reassure himself. "I'll go into the village to get more ingredients. Yes, I'll just have to make some more."

"Phew!" Charlotte breathed. "You scared me. I thought we drank the last of it." Humberly gave the girls a hard glare.

"You *did* drink the last of it," he snapped. "And that took a hundred years to make!"

"But I thought you said you could make more? Will we have to wait a hundred more years?" Mary glanced worriedly at Charlotte.

"No, of course not." Humberly softened. "I can make it in one day. It just won't be as potent, or predictable. The liquid you so brazenly consumed was of the highest quality." He looked at the girls. "You can expect to feel a bit, well, odd within the next few hours. It's probably best if you both stay here while I purchase the supplies."

Mary became nervous. "What exactly will it do to us?"

The fox cocked his head to the side. "The vanishing serum is designed to do exactly what it sounds like: make one disappear. Or in other words, it will make you invisible," he said plainly. "You and anything touching your skin."

The girls' mouths dropped open. "Now, don't worry too much. It should only last the night. I'm sure when you wake up you will have returned to normal."

"You mean, we'll get to be invisible for the rest of the day?" Charlotte asked excitedly.

"Yes. As I said, the serum was at its peak potency and designed to last for quite some time once it kicked in. This, of course, would have made it ideal for our upcoming journey," he added ruefully, "but alas, we will have to settle for a short and unpredictable version."

"Will it hurt?" Mary asked. "I mean, once it starts working?"

"Oh no, no. You may feel a bit tingly but that will be all. Now I must go. There is much to do."

"What should we do while you're gone?" Mary asked.

"Hmm, I suppose you could read." He gestured widely to the bookshelf. "It may do you good to learn more about Ilyor." Then he grabbed his satchel and a few empty vials from the desk drawer. "I will be back shortly. Try not to touch anything this time." With that, he pulled up the trap door and disappeared.

Charlotte and Mary looked at one another. "What have we gotten ourselves into?" Mary murmured.

"I don't know, but I can't wait to find out!"

"Aren't you afraid?"

"To be invisible? No way!" Charlotte grinned. "It will be awesome!"

Mary walked to the window and watched as Humberly left a lingering trail through the meadow. "But think of what might happen next."

Mary decided to take Humberly's advice and learn more about Ilyor, given she might be ruling it one day. Running her fingers along the spines, she noticed some of the volumes looked as though they were many centuries old. While she leafed through *The History of Ilyor*, Charlotte continued to rummage around the cottage. She moved random objects and ran her hands along the walls and floor hoping to find a switch to a hidden nook of some kind. *What else is hiding in this strange place?* she wondered.

Mary finished skimming and returned the volume to the shelf. As she was taking out another, the book appeared to be floating in midair. She jerked her hand away, letting it drop to the floor.

"Whoa! I guess it's working!" Charlotte said when she saw Mary's hand missing and the fallen hardback sprawled on the floor.

Mary wiggled her missing fingers. They seemed to work fine; she just couldn't see them. "I don't think I like this."

Charlotte got up to examine Mary's hand and looked down to see her own legs had vanished. "I'm floating!" she shouted excitedly.

"I'm glad one of us is happy."

As the serum continued to take effect, the room soon looked as though no one was there. Mary felt too strange to continue reading and began walking toward the chair. If she just sat down and closed her eyes she could pretend she didn't look like a ghost.

Instead, she crashed hard into something. Her glasses fell from her face as both girls cried out in unison.

"I guess it's better if only one person is invisible at a time," Mary concluded.

Charlotte rubbed her sore head. "You take the chair. I'll sit by the fire."

Once they were comfortable and the pain had subsided, their conversation turned toward the events of the day. It was hard to believe how different the morning was from the evening. Mary listened as Charlotte described the sensation of being hurled through the air and the satisfaction of discovering the secret door. By the excitement in her voice, Mary knew Charlotte was thrilled to be here. She, however, wasn't sure how she felt. She had always struggled to wrap her head around the peculiar - a trait probably passed down by her father. Needless to say, enchanted trees and talking animals were *definitely* peculiar.

She also couldn't fathom what it would be like to rule a kingdom. She fell silent as she questioned the idea that she was royalty. *How could I be the ruler of Ilyor? I didn't even know it existed until today. And I certainly don't know anything about ruling. Humberly has to be mistaken.*

Charlotte wondered why Mary was so quiet. "You haven't disappeared on me completely, have you?" she teased.

When she realized she hadn't responded to Charlotte's last question, Mary came out of her daze. "Sorry. I'm still here. What did you say?"

"I was just wondering if your dad had ever mentioned this place. You know, when he talked about your uncle."

"No. Not that I remember."

"What were you thinking about just now?"

"Oh, I don't know. It's hard to believe what Humberly said about me." Mary hesitated. "Do you really think it's true?"

"You mean about being an heir?" Charlotte was thoughtful for a moment. She didn't know if anything that was happening was even real, but she did know if any kid could rule a kingdom, it was Mary. "I don't think you need to worry about that," she said finally. "I'm sure you will know just what to do when the time comes."

Mary smiled at her friend's confidence. She wished she could be so sure. "And besides," Charlotte continued, "you'll always have me right by your side."

Mary felt the weight lessen. Even if she had no idea what she was doing, at least she didn't have to do it alone. "I wonder when Humberly will get back," she said, feeling more relaxed. She curled up in the armchair letting her eyes close.

Charlotte lay across the braided rug and peered out at the darkening sky. Even through the window, she could see the stars glowing brightly. "It sounded like he had a lot to do before tomorrow," she said as she smiled, thinking about what the morning might bring.

Mary murmured a response as she was falling asleep and Charlotte turned on her side to watch as the flames crackled and jumped. The heat wrapped around her like a heavy blanket, making her drowsy. "Please don't be a dream," she whispered before finally dozing off.

The next morning, Charlotte could hear pots and pans banging around in the kitchen. She buried her face into the pillow and groaned. If only she could slip back into her dream. But of course, Ilyor was too good to be true. Her thoughts drifted back to the exciting adventure she'd imagined. How she longed to be back in the Sycamore tree with Mary and Humberly, instead of in her room waiting for her brothers to jolt her awake.

The sharp sound of whistling flooded the room, making Charlotte wonder. *No one in my family whistles.* Finally, she made herself turn over. Relief swept over her when she saw Humberly preparing a large pot of stew.

"Good morning, Sunshine!" Mary called.

Charlotte sat up. "We're still here! And you're not invisible anymore!"

Mary laughed. "Neither are you."

Charlotte noticed the peeling green nail polish on her nails and smiled. She could see her hands again. She threw off the blanket and jumped up. She couldn't wait to get started. As Humberly set the pot over the fire, he looked about the cottage.

"I hope you girls don't leave your beds like this at home." Charlotte and Mary glanced at the blankets and pillows scattered over the armchair and floor.

Mary flushed. "Sorry, Humberly." They began to straighten the bedding. "Where did these come from anyway? We didn't have them last night."

Humberly continued to stir the pot. "This cottage holds more than you think," he explained. He set the ladle down and took the bedding. "You just have to know where to look." Walking to the far wall, he ran his hand over the smooth wood. Suddenly, a narrow door opened revealing an inner room.

Charlotte gasped wondering how she'd missed that yesterday. Peering inside, she saw that Humberly was right. The room held almost every household item she could think of. Pots, pans, blankets, and old clothing lined the shelves while various fruits, vegetables, and things they'd never seen before sat in baskets in a corner.

"How is that possible?" Mary asked. "The tree isn't wide enough to have this much room."

"Magic," Humberly said wistfully. "Everything in this Sycamore is enchanted." He returned the blankets to the shelf and closed the door. "You must have noticed when the fireplace came to life."

"We still haven't figured out how that happened," Charlotte admitted.

"When someone sits in the armchair, the fire is instantly ignited. When it's cold enough in the room, that is."

Realization dawned on Mary and Charlotte.

"Now, who's hungry?" Humberly set three places at the table and ladled stew into each bowl.

"I don't think I've ever had stew for breakfast before," Charlotte commented, taking her first bite. "And I know I've never tasted stew like this before!"

Mary's eyes grew wide in agreement as she sampled the hearty meal. The unusual spices paired perfectly with the simmered roast.

"A nourishing breakfast for a hard journey," Humberly remarked modestly. After breakfast, he pulled a large bundle from his satchel. "You must also dress properly before we go." He handed each girl a package wrapped in fine linen.

Charlotte ran her fingers over the smooth parcel before untying the satin ribbon. As the wrapping fell away, she let out a small gasp. Inside was the most beautiful clothing she'd ever seen. She stroked the pair of fine leather, button-up boots. They were obviously made with great care, as the black threaded seams were flawless.

Setting the boots aside, she held up a ruby dress. The soft, velvety fabric slid between her fingers. Traces of silver thread were sewn throughout the otherwise seamless dress, and a thick strip of silver, studded with small rubies, bordered the hem and each fitted sleeve.

Charlotte stared at the dress in awe. Eventually, she forced herself to look at Mary, who was busy admiring her own exquisite clothing. Mary's dress was similar to her own but made of royal purple, with dashes of golden thread peeking through. Instead of rubies, the golden border was lined with small diamonds. Charlotte thought Mary's dress was just as stunning as her own. Suddenly, she had a hunch. "Humberly, did you make these?"

"I thought you would be pleased." He motioned toward the pantry. "Now, go change out of those... er, garments." He finished, unable to suppress a slight look of contempt.

"I can see why the king was angry when you left," Charlotte remarked before stepping into the pantry with Mary. The girls couldn't wait to try on the new dresses. They helped one another with the long row of buttons on the back of each dress. "Have you ever felt more beautiful?" Mary asked, caressing her velvety sleeve.

Charlotte smiled as she opened the door.

"Ah, now that's better." Humberly handed each girl a small leather satchel. "Here are some provisions for our journey." The girls relished the hand-sewn satchels while Humberly picked up his bag.

When they were ready, he regarded them seriously. "Now, before we begin, there is something you must remember. When the king discovers you are here, he will stop at nothing to prevent you from finding the crown. The king's henchmen are masters of deceit. They will come in all forms to tempt you to despair. You must hold fast to the truth. You are the heir. They are the counterfeit. Always be on your guard."

A shudder ran down Mary's spine at the thought of now having enemies. She watched as Charlotte followed Humberly through the trap door. Taking a deep breath, she steadied her nerves and focused on Humberly's words. But no matter how hard she tried, she couldn't shake the feeling that *she* was the counterfeit.

Chapter Eight

Gloomy Beginnings

W hen they made it to the bottom of the stairwell, Humberly closed the door behind him and advised them to step away from the tree. In a moment or so, as fast as it had grown, the tree shrank back to its normal height. Watching from the safety of the ground was much more appealing.

Charlotte reached into her dress pocket but found it empty. "Don't worry," Humberly said. "The key is back where you found it."

"But how?"

"You'll understand this world better with time." At that, he turned around and led them through the meadow in the direction the girls were headed before the tree revealed its magic to them. Charlotte ran her hand along the soft petals as they stretched up toward her fingertips.

Crossing an old cobblestone bridge, Humberly bent down in front of a glistening bush. He took a glass vial from his satchel and held it to the tip of a leaf. "It's best to get this ingredient as fresh as possible," he said. As he blew on the leaf, a sap-like substance began to drip into the vial. Charlotte and Mary stared in amazement.

"What is that?" they asked in unison.

"It's called Armoracite. The leaves of this bush are covered in a sticky film. When hot air touches them, the substance releases, becoming a liquid."

"What is it for?" Mary questioned.

"It's typically used as a skin armor, but it can also be used to coat objects like glass or wood. Anything breakable."

"What do you mean by *skin armor*?" Charlotte wanted to know. Not taking his eyes off of what he was doing, Humberly explained.

"When you rub the oil onto your skin, it forms a barrier making your skin impenetrable. Similar to wearing a suit of armor. Hence the name 'Armoracite'."

"Can I try it?" Charlotte asked enthusiastically.

"All in good time." Humberly closed the lid of the vial. The girls watched in awe as he filled multiple bottles with the shiny sap. After finishing his work, he returned the vials to his satchel. "Now we're ready for the swamp."

"Swamp?" Mary asked. "As in crocodiles and slimy things?"

"Crocodiles? No. I don't believe we have those here. I'm not aware of any slimy things, either."

"That's a relief."

"I'm sure," Humberly replied. He led the girls beneath the tall trees, deeper into the forest. "We just have to watch out for the five-horned serpent living in the acidic waters. One bite can kill a grown man instantly."

A look of panic spread across Mary's face. "Is that all?" Charlotte asked sarcastically. She gave Mary a gentle nudge. "Don't worry, we just have to stay out of the water. How hard can that be?"

Mary smiled weakly. "I think I'd rather face a crocodile."

The narrow path wound tightly through the forest. Bright green leaves swayed in the breeze and small animals ducked in and out of their homes. The trio hiked over fallen logs and passed through hanging vines. After walking in silence for some time, Charlotte couldn't keep quiet any longer. She had to know more.

"What was it like?" she asked. "Finding the first gem? Did you almost die?" She hadn't meant to sound so excited about this last question.

"Ahh, that is quite a story," he replied. "And I suppose we did come rather close to losing our lives. Sir Richard and I had the most difficult time," he said with a smile as the memory came back to him. "You see, each gem is hidden in a region of darkness. If they were hidden in areas of light, the gems would quickly reveal themselves to restore all of nature to its former glory.

"Sir Richard and I knew it would be a dangerous task when we first saw that the map of the gems' locations led to the rocky cliffs of Aramanthia; a dreadful place with jagged peaks and hidden crevices.

"We were determined, however, to retrieve what had been lost. Traveling quickly, it took two days to reach the edge of the canyon. I remember seeing the cliffs once before as a child. They had terrified me then, but this time was somehow worse. It was as though the darkness knew why we were there. A long shadow crept across the floor of the ravine, awakening everything in its path. I shuddered as I saw the earth quake at its touch.

"There was little time for fear, though, so we quickly secured a rope and lowered ourselves down. The crumbling wall caused us to frequently lose our grip. If not for the security of the rope, I don't know what would have become of us. It was a long, tedious descent into the abyss, but once on the ground, there was some relief in being far from the needle-like rocks above.

"The ground, however, continued to break apart as the shadow passed over. We tried our best to stay off of its path but it spread quickly. We had to run down narrow stretches of earth until we reached a towering rock formation in the center of the chasm. Sir Richard was sure the gem would be hidden there. He seemed to sense its presence, as I'm sure you have as well, Mary."

Mary nodded soberly and Humberly continued.

"The trench of surrounding lava jumped and spat, knowing full well we didn't belong. We coated as much of your uncle as we could in Armoracite before he climbed a tall boulder and stretched himself across the narrow ledge. Try as it might, the lava could not scorch his skin.

When he was close enough to the center, he could see the gem tucked safely within the nook. "It's here!" he shouted down to me.

I howled with joy. I could hardly believe it. It felt as though Ilyor finally had real hope. Then it began to glow, just as it did for Mary, only not quite as bright." He threw a look of confidence toward her before continuing.

"I remember we were both in awe when we saw the gem reveal its secret prison. Sir Richard later admitted he'd been transfixed by the sight of it; that he couldn't have left it even if he wanted to. When it came time to remove the jewel, though, it refused to budge. After centuries of being wedged into place, the rock had begun to grow around it. Sir Richard took a small pick out of his satchel and carefully chipped away at the surrounding pillar. Slowly, the gem came loose.

You can't imagine the thrill of our success. Sir Richard brought the gem to me and we pranced around like children, whooping and hollering." Humberly laughed. "I don't think I'd ever been more excited." He paused to wipe his eyes.

"Our celebration didn't last long, however. Shortly after the gem was removed, the ground shook with tremendous force and the cliffs began to collapse. Sir Richard tucked the jewel into the inner part of his satchel and we raced across the ravine, having a difficult time staying upright. Hot steam shot up from every crater, marking us with blisters if it came too close.

We reached the wall with speed we did not have on our way down. Thankfully, the rope was still intact. Sir Richard had already reached the top when the earth gave way beneath my feet. I lost hold of the rope and skidded down the coarse wall, grasping for anything I could find.

My hand finally caught a ridge, and I held on for dear life. The lava was quickly rising as the canyon floor disappeared beneath me. If not for your uncle throwing the rope at me, I would have been consumed. As soon as I scrambled to the top, we ran through the woods until our legs gave out." Humberly ended with a soft chuckle and tossed the stick he'd been fiddling with into the woods. "If only he could be here now."

Mary's heart ached. Humberly had lost his closest friend. She couldn't imagine what it would be like to lose Charlotte. Everything would be different. She quickly pushed the thought aside, not wanting to dwell on it.

Charlotte let out a long whistle. "I hope we get an adventure like that!"

"We'll have our own sort of adventure, I'm sure," Humberly said. His story had so thoroughly captivated the girls that they hardly noticed the scenery around them had changed. The once bright, flourishing forest now looked dark and ominous.

"Are you sure we're going the right way?" Mary asked, hoping they had simply taken a wrong turn.

"This is the way." Humberly seemed completely unfazed by their surroundings. "We only need to round this bend."

Mary's stomach tightened. *I hope we don't meet the serpent,* she thought. She was almost certain, though, that the serpent was the reason for this gem's hiding place.

As they rounded the corner, Charlotte thought the swamp wasn't nearly as bad as she expected. Most everything was wet, dirty, and brown, but at least there weren't any creatures lurking about. At least none that she could see.

Humberly walked right up to the edge of the marsh. "Now remember, the most dangerous area is the water. I imagine the gem will be hidden somewhere in there." Mary's eyes widened.

"Will we have to go into the water to find it?" she asked in horror.

"Heavens, no. This water cannot touch any part of our bodies. The acidity alone would kill us. We can use the lily pads to walk across. Mary, since the gem only glows when you're near, you must lead the way." Mary's face grew pale.

"Don't worry. The serpent will only come out if the waters are disturbed. Now, step onto this first pad and tell me what you see."

Mary felt her knees weaken. *He can't be serious.* The look on his face, however, told her otherwise. She felt Charlotte's hand on her back.

"We'll be right behind you."

She nodded slightly before reluctantly walking to the edge of the water. If this is what it meant to be a queen, she was sure she didn't want to be one.

Setting one foot on the large pad, she grimaced as her weight shifted. But the pad was surprisingly sturdy. Even as she stood on both feet, it remained perfectly still. She heaved a sigh of relief before drawing up enough courage to look into the murky water. "The water's too dark. I can't see anything."

"That's alright," Humberly reassured her. "I'm sure you'll see it when it starts to glow. Now, move along." Mary timidly stepped from one lily pad to the next. Humberly trailed behind her, followed by Charlotte. They were halfway across the swamp when a soft blue glow came from below the surface. As she drew nearer, the glow brightened.

"I think I see it!" she cried out excitedly. Humberly stepped beside her for a closer look.

"I believe you're right." He patted her on the shoulder. "Now, we just have to get it out."

"Maybe we can scoop it out with a couple of sticks," Charlotte said.

Humberly thought for a moment. "Once we disturb the waters, we won't have much time. It doesn't appear to be far from the surface. I believe it will be best to grab it ourselves and not take the chance of it slipping down farther."

"How will we do that if we can't touch the water?" Mary asked.

Humberly took the Armoracite from his satchel. "I will coat your arms so you can retrieve the gem unharmed."

Mary's mouth dropped open. "Why do I have to do it? You can see the gem as much as I can."

"Charlotte and I must distract the serpent. You have to stay near the gem so it continues to glow."

"I'm sorry, did you say 'distract the serpent'?" Charlotte interrupted. Mary opened her mouth but then closed it. Retrieving the gem had to be easier than diverting a serpent. Even if the waters *were* deadly.

Humberly opened the vial as Mary held out both arms. "Charlotte, you and I will first disturb the waters near the edge of the pond," he explained. "We will need to lure the serpent onto land so it is nowhere near Mary."

"What about us?" Charlotte exclaimed. "Who will lure it away from us?"

Ignoring Charlotte's panic, Humberly finished coating Mary's arms. Mary could feel the sticky sap begin to solidify. "Be ready to grab the gem but don't do anything until I say," Humberly commanded.

"You don't have to worry about that."

Humberly stepped past Charlotte and she followed him back across the pond. "Now," he began, "when the serpent is on land, he will only return to the water if he knows we do not have the gem."

"So, we just tell him we don't have it?" Charlotte asked skeptically.

"Not quite. Once Mary has secured the gem and is safely out of harm's way, I will throw this large stone into the water. As long as he doesn't notice Mary, he will think the gem is safely back in its hideout."

"But the stone doesn't glow. He'll know it's not the real thing."

"The serpent doesn't know the gem glows," he reminded her. "Snakes in general are naturally color blind. We just have to hope *he* is too."

Charlotte let the information sink in. "Okay," she said slowly. She could feel her stomach clench and her palms started to sweat. It was both thrilling and terrifying to be getting her wish.

Adventure seemed so easy in her imagination. But in reality, she needed to distract a serpent from a magical gem in just a few moments. Something she never thought she'd have to do.

"How do we even distract him?" she finally asked.

"Simple. We run." Charlotte waited for Humberly to continue. When he remained silent, her eyes widened.

"That's it? No offense, but I don't think that's the best plan." She looked to Mary for support but she was too far across the swamp to hear. "Shouldn't we at least coat ourselves in Armoracite too?"

"That won't be necessary," Humberly assured her. "Just stick to the plan."

"Right. Just run."

"And fast," Humberly added. "Are you ready?" Charlotte took a deep breath.

"As ready as I'll ever be."

Chapter Nine

The Invisible Man

Humberly found several long sticks and, standing as far back from the pond as possible, began to stir the edge of the water. He was right about the acidity. Charlotte watched as each stick was eaten away. The bundle of wood dwindled, but the water remained still.

Finally, after collecting a few more sticks, Charlotte thought she saw something move. She stared hard at the surface. Just when she decided she'd been mistaken, a round body, at least a foot across, glided along the surface. "There it is!" she squealed, more loudly than she meant to. The serpent had to be at least ten feet long by the time she saw the tale.

"I see it," Humberly replied evenly. "Step back and be ready."

Charlotte's whole body tensed. She waited nervously for the snake to come closer. It took its time, seemingly sizing up its enemies. The sharp horns lining its back protruded from the water momentarily before sinking out of sight.

Then the water went perfectly still.

Charlotte scanned the surface frantically.

"Where is it?"

Humberly kept his eyes fixed on the edge of the swamp. Charlotte had just taken a step forward when he suddenly dropped the stick and shouted: "Run!"

The serpent lurched forward. Humberly grabbed Charlotte's arm and pulled her alongside him. "Mary now!"

Mary reached into the water as Charlotte's legs sprang into action. The serpent was even faster than she expected. They hurdled fallen logs and dodged bushes and tree trunks. It didn't matter where they ended up, as long as they could outrun the monster chasing them. Now, leading the way, she thought she'd even outrun Humberly. But glancing back, she found him right at her heels. "Keep going!" he shouted.

Turning back around, her foot caught a root which sent her flying through the air. It seemed an eternity before she crashed hard onto the ground. Stunned, she braced herself for the sharp fangs, but they never came.

Acting quickly, Humberly threw something yellow at the snake before pulling her to her feet. It sputtered and stalled for a few precious seconds, allowing her to regain her momentum. She gave no thought to the throbbing in her knee as she sprinted to keep up with the swift fox.

It wasn't long before it was close behind them again. They could hear the rushing of its body over the dry brush. As Humberly kept the lead and circled back toward the pond, the snake continued to slither over everything in its path, not losing an inch. He took the stone from his pocket, holding it out for the viper to see. Charlotte didn't believe it would work until she heard a terrifying hiss, making it clear the snake not only believed the stone was the gem but it was also determined to retrieve it.

When they were finally close enough, he threw the stone as hard as he could into the water. The snake let out one last threatening hiss before veering away to reclaim the false gem. All at once, everything was quiet.

They made sure they were far away before stopping to catch their breath. "I've never run so hard in my life," Charlotte said, gasping. "How did you keep the snake from biting me?"

Humberly took a second to recover before showing her the yellow pow-der. "Stunning powder. I kept it in my pocket just in case." She shuddered to think what could've happened otherwise. Suddenly, a twig snapped behind them and the duo jumped.

"Sorry," Mary said.

Charlotte let out a sigh of relief. "I'm just glad it's you. Please tell me you got it."

Mary held out her hand and smiled. The second gem was just as beau-tiful as the first. They all admired the stunning sapphire.

"That was well worth the effort," Humberly chimed. "Well done, girls." Even Charlotte had to agree. Finally, he took the gem from Mary and slid it into a secure pouch in his satchel.

"The next gem is about ten miles away, near the village."

"Ten miles?" Charlotte and Mary asked in unison.

"I don't think I can walk that far. I'm exhausted from all of that run-ning," Charlotte complained.

"I'm sure you'll have plenty of energy. The stew you ate this morning will help. Plus, you'll find your boots are made for such a trek."

"Are they enchanted to do the walking for me?" Charlotte asked hope-fully.

"Not quite. But they are rather comfortable if I do say so myself." The girls couldn't argue with that. Everything Humberly made seemed to be of the highest quality. He began walking, leaving them to reluctantly trail behind.

The air grew chillier as they made their way into the mountains. After walking for miles, they finally took a break to put on the cloaks Humberly had packed.

"Is it always this cold?" Charlotte asked.

"Only in the early mornings and evenings. The days are quite beautiful this time of year."

They went another few miles before Charlotte's stomach started to grumble. She could tell the stew was beginning to wear off. Humberly must have noticed because he turned his head and said, "Just a little farther."

Just as he predicted, houses began popping up sporadically. Quaint stone cottages with smoke pluming from the chimneys dotted the lane. Mary thought she'd very much like to live in one of these cozy cottages.

Eventually, the dirt path turned into gravel. Houses of various sizes lined the road and people and animals briskly went about their business. No one seemed to pay any mind to the trio as they made their way to the center of town.

Mary and Charlotte stayed close to Humberly as they took in their surroundings. The village made it seem as though they'd gone back in time. Storefronts stood in rows on either side of the street, and horses clopped along, pulling old-fashioned buggies. They found it hard not to stare at the unfamiliar sights.

In the middle of town, they came to a tavern where Humberly stopped in front of the large wooden door. Long, rose-colored windows flanked the entrance on either side. "We'll rest here for a bit and be on our way," Humberly said.

"Will we have to walk more today?" Mary asked.

Humberly studied the worn-out pair. The girls were disheveled and exhausted. He glanced at the sinking sun. "It did take us longer than I expected to get here." He furrowed his brow as he thought. "I suppose we can stay for the night."

Relief swept over the girls. "But, we must be up at dawn to locate the third gem and move on to the next," Humberly finished.

"No more swamps, I hope?" Mary questioned.

"No, nothing like that," he replied, giving no hint of what they might face.

Humberly pushed his whole body against the heavy tavern door. It slowly creaked open, releasing a heavenly scent. Inside, the tavern was furnished with low wooden tables and large fireplaces. It was comfortable and warm compared to the chilly evening air. Wooden stools lined the bar and waitresses scurried around, delivering warm drinks and large trays of food.

A plump woman with rosy cheeks and bright eyes rushed over to greet them. "Ooh, Humberly!" she cried, wiping her hands on her apron. "How good it is to see you!" She smiled at the girls warmly and leaned back with her hands on her hips. "And who are these lovely ladies?"

"Maribel, I'd like you to meet Mary and Charlotte. They're accompanying me on a... journey."

"Oh! Good to meet you. Come, have a seat. I'll have you all set in no time." She patted the table before disappearing as quickly as she came.

Mary and Charlotte made themselves comfortable at the crudely carved table. It had been a long day, and they were happy to relax in the warm room. Most of the guests were eating merrily, while some were tramping to and from the second floor. The girls were glad they would be staying for the night. It had been such a strange day.

Soon, Maribel was back with three goblets and a tray full of delicious-looking food. She set a place before each of them and again hurried away. "Thank you," Humberly called after her. "Maribel is the kindest woman you will ever meet, but if you want to talk to her, you have to be quick!" he said with a chuckle.

Charlotte's eyes grew wide as she surveyed the assortment of food. The tray was filled with roasted potatoes, seared vegetables, baked ham, steaming roast beef, bread and butter, and all kinds of fruit she'd never seen before. She wanted to try some of everything. Humberly picked up the crisp loaf of bread and began breaking it apart.

Mary was just as hungry as the others and hurriedly filled her plate. As she took her first bite, her gaze wandered to the corner of the room where she saw a shadowy figure staring intently at her. She shifted uncomfortably trying not to stare back.

Hoping she'd been mistaken, she glanced over again only to find his eyes still fixated on her. She tried to conceal her discomfort and pretended not to notice. When the waiter had his attention, though, she strained to get a better look. The hunched figure seemed smaller than average, but that was all she could tell apart from the dark hood.

"Humberly," she whispered.

"Yes?" Humberly continued to spread butter across a large piece of bread.

"Do you know that man?"

Humberly looked over. "The one leaning against the wall?" Mary followed his gaze to a large man gulping his drink and belching loudly.

"No, the man on the last bar stool." She nodded toward the figure who had once again turned toward the bar.

"There's no one on the last bar stool."

"What do you mean?" Mary objected. "He's right there. In the black hood." Humberly once again turned from his bread and searched the corner. After looking around thoroughly, he turned back to Mary.

"Are you feeling alright?"

"Of course," Mary responded irritably. "Why? Can't you see him now?"

Humberly gave her a sympathetic look. "The bar stool is still empty, dear. Why don't you try eating something? It's been a long day."

Mary opened her mouth to protest, but when she looked back at the counter the man was gone. "Oh. I guess he left," she mumbled. She wasn't sure if her mind was playing tricks on her or if Humberly just needed glasses. She tried to forget about the figure and continue eating, but no matter how hard she tried, she couldn't shake the ominous feeling growing inside of her.

Chapter Ten

Enticement

The trio ate until satisfied and then enjoyed their cider while unwinding from the events of the day. Charlotte still couldn't believe she'd outrun what looked to be an overgrown python. She laughed to herself thinking of how loudly she'd squealed when it first came out of the water.

Humberly ordered one more round of cider. He could see that both Charlotte and Mary had finally begun to relax. He held his glass up. "Cheers, girls," he said. "You can be proud of the job you did today." Mary and Charlotte smiled. It was refreshing to hear the confidence in his voice.

As the sun disappeared behind the mountain, he arranged for their rooms and sent the girls straight to bed. Feeling relieved to be staying the night, they gladly climbed the stairs and walked to their room. "Get some sleep. We'll be heading out at the crack of dawn," Humberly reminded them for the third time that evening. He then went to his room across the hall.

The key clicked in the lock and the stiff door creaked as it opened. Mary set the candle on the side table and looked around. Other than being somewhat outdated, the small room felt cozy. A warm fire blazed in the hearth, and a plump queen-sized bed drew both of their attention. Charlotte leaped forward and sprawled out on the dark green comforter.

"Ah, that's better. My legs can't take another step." Mary brought their bags to the nightstand. Inside, she found two sets of thermals. After handing Charlotte one, she quickly changed into her own and hopped into bed. Charlotte had already snuggled deep under the covers. "I could sleep in this bed for the rest of my life," she stated.

"When we become royalty, our first order of business will be to move this bed into the castle," Mary joked.

"You mean when *you* become royalty," Charlotte corrected. "I'll just be a lowly peasant following you around like a puppy dog."

"Then my first order will be to make you royalty, too."

"I don't think it works that way." Charlotte laughed.

Mary figured she was kidding, but she also wondered if Charlotte believed there was truth in what she said.

"What do you think it will be like to live in a castle anyway?" Charlotte asked. "Having servants who do everything for you?"

Mary thought for a second. "I don't know if I'd ever get used to it. It wouldn't be anything like home. My mom would ground me for a month if I ordered her to clean my room." Charlotte smiled as she pictured the look on Mrs. Albright's face if Mary ordered her around.

Mary let out a long yawn and nestled into her pillow. She tried to keep her eyelids open, but they were as heavy as lead. Charlotte could tell her friend was about to fall asleep and didn't ask any more questions. Her own body was worn out, and she knew she needed rest too, so she rolled over and shut her eyes. But even when she tried to relax, she couldn't keep her thoughts from drifting to the future. A future where she'd not only be replaced by a new baby but possibly left behind by her best friend as well.

Charlotte awoke early to the sound of thunder and heavy rain pounding the roof. She quickly yanked the blankets up to her chin. The air in the room was freezing cold now that the fire had gone out. Mary lay awake beside her staring at the ceiling. "Do you think the fire will light on its own like it does at the tree house?" Mary asked.

"I doubt it. If it was enchanted, it wouldn't have gone out in the first place."

A soft knock sounded at the door. The chilly wooden floor was far too cold to touch. "Come in!" Charlotte called from across the room. The door creaked open and Humberly's long snout appeared. He peeked in to greet them and saw they were still bundled up in bed.

"Would you like a fire?" he asked. Charlotte and Mary were relieved.

"Yes, please," they answered in unison. It only took him a few minutes to get the fire blazing again.

"I assume you've noticed it's past the crack of dawn."

"It's hard to tell with the storm," Charlotte admitted.

"Yes, it's quite unruly out there. I hate to do it but we'll have to delay our journey until it passes. I'm afraid we wouldn't get very far in this weather."

Mary sighed. She still wasn't sure if she wanted to be queen, but now that she knew the allure of the gems, she felt drawn to find everyone.

"Now, get dressed and come to breakfast. Maribel makes the most delicious flapjacks." He turned to go downstairs.

Mary looked at Charlotte. "What are flapjacks?"

"I don't know," Charlotte said, hopping out of bed. "Let's go find out."

The girls stood near the fire for a few minutes before getting dressed. When they went downstairs, Humberly was waiting for them at a large table with heaping stacks of buttery pancakes in the center. Fresh strawberry jam and honey butter sat in mason jars while sizzling sausages and fried eggs were being warmed in a skillet. Toasted bread and a large cup of hot apple cider were near each plate.

The girls eagerly sat down. Charlotte leaned in and took a deep breath. The smells made her mouth water. "It reminds me of Mary's house on a Saturday morning."

Mary had the same thought. Instead of comforting, though, the big breakfast made her feel homesick. She pictured her family sitting around the table together and felt as though she'd already been gone a month.

"Eat up before it gets cold," Humberly said. "Wouldn't want to insult the cook." The events of the previous day gave Mary and Charlotte healthy appetites. When they finished eating, they thanked Maribel, who had come to clear their plates.

"What should we do until the storm clears?" Charlotte asked.

"Well," Humberly started, "since we can't hunt for gems, you may as well explore the village. It will do you good to get to know the townspeople." He withdrew a few small stones from his pouch and the girls looked at each other excitedly. "Your cloaks will help keep you dry. But be sure to stay away from the Northern part of the village. We will eventually end up there, but it's not safe to go alone."

The girls readily accepted the small stones and ran upstairs to get their cloaks. Wrapping themselves in the hooded robes, they opened the tavern door and darted into the rain. The wind whipped around them and they pulled their wraps tightly around their bodies.

Across the street, a covered walkway offered shelter. A mixture of meat and strong seasonings drifted toward them as they stood near the open door of the butcher shop. A variety of meats hung from hooks on the ceiling and the large butcher moved quickly behind the counter preparing orders. He hummed in a deep voice as he worked.

They moved past the general store and livery until they came to a shop surrounded by clematis vines. When Mary opened the door, a small bell chimed and the smell of lavender greeted them. The girls were instantly drawn to the store's charm.

Inside, they saw rich fabrics cascading down walls, ornate bottles of colorful perfumes, and an assortment of spices lining the shelf above a counter of jewelry. Their fascination was soon interrupted by a friendly welcome.

"Hello, ladies. I was wondering when you'd stop by." A petite older woman with long, graying blonde hair stepped from behind the counter. She wore a deep purple skirt that went down to her boots and swished back and forth as she walked.

Before Charlotte could ask, the woman answered her question.

"I saw you come into town yesterday. I knew my shop would draw you in. I'm Annabel."

As Mary was about to answer, Annabel held up her hand. "Let me guess. You're Mary," she said correctly, "and you must be Charlotte."

"How did you know?" Mary asked.

Annabel waved her hand dismissively. "Oh, word gets around. You know how small towns can be. Now, is there anything I can help you find?"

Charlotte wasn't sure she knew how small towns could be, but she brushed away the uncertainty. "We're just seeing what Ilyor has to offer."

"I thought you might not be from around here. What brings you to Ilyor?"

Neither girl was sure how to answer. Finally, Mary replied. "We're here with our friend, Humberly."

The owner waited for more, but when they revealed nothing further she went on. "I'm sure you'll learn all about Ilyor and more with Humberly as your guide." Charlotte thought she saw a flicker in the woman's eyes.

"Let me show you some of the pieces we have to offer." Annabel led the girls around, pointing out velvety fabrics and exquisite handmade jewelry. "These jewels were all mined from the Crescent Mountain. Some say they're magical." The girls admired the rare stones. Then Annabel led them to the shelves of spices. Some smelled wonderful, while others were more pungent. The pungent ones reminded Charlotte of her brother's dirty socks but she kept her thoughts to herself.

Eventually, Mary picked out a beautiful jade scarf to purchase, and they decided to move on. "Before you go, I have something for you." Annabel stepped behind the counter. "I can tell there's something special about the two of you." She held out a small brooch on display. "This is for you." She handed it to Mary.

"This is beautiful, but I doubt I can afford it."

"Don't worry, darling. It's a gift. The stone is from the mountain I was telling you about earlier. This brooch will warn you when danger is near." She walked over to the perfume display.

"And I'd like you to have this." She handed a round turquoise bottle to Charlotte.

"Thank you," she said, opening the bottle. "It smells lovely."

"This is not just a perfume. It also has the power of persuasion. Spray it on someone, and they will immediately do as you say. You will only need a small amount."

Charlotte was skeptical. "So, you're saying I can use this to make people do whatever I want?"

"Yes." She smiled. "But be sure to use it wisely."

Charlotte promised and they thanked Annabel before stepping onto the platform. The rain was still falling heavily.

Mary pinned her brooch to her cloak. "What do you think?"

"Looks good." Charlotte turned the perfume over in her hand. "Did Annabel seem a little *different* to you?"

"Maybe a little. But it was nice of her to give us gifts."

Nodding, Charlotte glanced back toward the store and was alarmed to see Annabel watching them. Aware she'd been spotted, Annabel smiled sheepishly and disappeared. Charlotte's brow furrowed. "Let's go." She turned and hurried along the walkway, leaving Mary to catch up.

The girls spent the next hour exploring shops and meeting villagers. They were sorry to learn of the hardships the residents suffered under the king's reign. Many had been forced to leave everything they had when their region was taken over. Not only did the king take whatever he pleased, but as his power grew, the darkness spread like a virus, killing crops and destroying their livelihoods. Those who fought back were either killed or imprisoned in the castle dungeons. Only a few regions have escaped the king's control. At least for now.

Mary felt both saddened and overwhelmed. *The villagers didn't deserve to be treated this way, but how was she supposed to stop a king who was so evil?* Even if they did find all of the gems, it would still be up to her to call on the Meir and then rule a kingdom. This seemed like an impossible task. She was only a child after all. And right now she just wanted to run home and hide under the covers. Being the only heir in Ilyor was too much.

She took a step back to clear her head, letting Charlotte lead the conversation with the bakery owner's daughter. Going to the store window and inhaling the crisp air, she realized how easy it'd be to leave Ilyor and never return. A large part of her was tempted to grab Charlotte and run before Humberly even noticed. Maybe she'd even convince her dad to come and help the people. Then she wouldn't feel guilty leaving. *I'm sure he'd believe in Ilyor if I brought him to the tree of enchantment,* she thought. He could summon the Meir and then put someone else in charge. There had to be a distant cousin or a great-aunt who could wear the crown. The more she thought about it, the better the idea seemed.

In a flurry of nerves, she turned to signal her friend but stopped short. Charlotte was completely consumed in her conversation with the baker's daughter. The girl appeared to be sharing something troubling, given the fiery look in Charlotte's eyes. After a moment, Charlotte laid a hand on the girl's arm and said something. The girl looked up with a soft smile before getting up to go behind the counter.

Charlotte always has a way of making people feel better, Mary thought. Being reminded of this made Mary feel less defeated. Charlotte was rarely intimidated by the worries of life, and her strength and kindness were something Mary could rely on even when things were hard.

Mary sat down at the table just as the girl, Eva, returned with an assortment of baked goods. "These are our specialties," she said with a strange accent. The flaky treats melted in their mouths as they continued their conversation. Eva had just shared that her grandfather's land was recently taken over by the king.

"He lost everything he owned and was nearly imprisoned for daring to fight back," she shared. "I worry that our town will be next. The Meir's power is stretched thin already. Once the king takes over, who knows what will happen to us."

Mary could hear the pain in Eva's voice as Charlotte glanced at her with a look of concern. At that moment, Mary knew she couldn't give up. And neither *should* she. The villagers had experienced enough sorrow. Even if she failed, which she thought was likely, she had to at least try.

After saying goodbye to Eva, they wandered along the dirt road. The rain had turned to a drizzle and a cool humidity settled in. They made it to the edge of town when a translucent butterfly fluttered past Mary's ear. The two admired the creature as it glided around them.

Mesmerized, they followed the butterfly through a mass of trees. The thick canopy blocked any stray drops of rain from reaching them. The trail eventually opened to a clearing in which the butterfly joined a multitude of others. The girls gasped at the sight. "It's incredible!" Mary breathed. They giggled as the insects landed on their heads and flitted about in front of them.

As one rested gently on Charlotte's hand, opening and closing its pale wings, a drop of water touched its back, causing a flash of magenta to travel through its body. The girls stood in awe, observing the dozens of butterflies momentarily changing from clear, to shades of blues, greens, and reds.

They weren't sure how long they stood admiring the symphony of colors, but when the rain finally let up the butterflies rose as a group and flew back into the forest. Watching until they were out of sight, the girls shaded their eyes from the now glaring sun.

"I think we're in a fairy tale," Mary sighed. Charlotte agreed while taking in the landscape around them for the first time. Though hazy, the outline of a large mountain could be seen in the distant north, while rolling hills stretched toward the west as far as the eye could see. She took in the scenery with a deep sense of contentment. Then a striking sight caught her eye.

"Mary, look at that tree."

Mary glanced to where she was pointing. "That's almost as pretty as the Sycamore."

Within a few minutes, they were underneath the tree's low hanging limbs. Its branches were covered in bright yellow leaves and held an abundance of deep purple fruit. The fruit looked so enticing it made their mouths water.

"I wasn't hungry until I saw *this*." Charlotte snatched a piece from a nearby branch and greedily took a bite. The sweet, tangy punch of a pomegranate mixed with a hint of rich blackberry overwhelmed her taste buds. Her eyes grew wide as the pink juice dribbled down her chin. "This is even better than Humberly's stew."

Mary eagerly grabbed a piece for herself. The pair couldn't believe their luck as they thoroughly enjoyed their new treat. It didn't seem like they could ever get enough. Finishing her first one, Charlotte dropped the pit to the ground and reached for another.

Suddenly, a twinge of pain made her recoil. A bitter aftertaste crept into her throat while her insides twisted into knots. She fell to her knees and groaned. "Something's not right, Mary."

Surprised by her friend's sudden agony, Mary dropped down beside her, unsure how to help. She opened her satchel, hoping to find something useful until the same pain overtook her. She doubled over beside Charlotte. "What's going on?" she managed to say with a moan.

Charlotte was in too much anguish to respond. She leaned against the tree thinking she was going to be sick. She almost hoped she would be. It might make her feel better.

Curling into a ball, she watched as a thick mist slowly settled over the land. It wrapped itself around her like a smothering blanket, making her drowsy.

While she fought to keep her eyes open, a dim silhouette appeared through the fog. At first, it seemed like a shadow. But as she watched, the shape transformed into the outline of a man moving toward her. Unable to fight it any longer, she reluctantly fell into a deep sleep.

Chapter Eleven

Doubts and Insecurities

Charlotte woke to her head throbbing. She felt extremely irritable and her mouth was dry like the desert. But at least the sourness in her stomach had subsided. Mary was still sound asleep so she decided not to wake her. The longing to find water motivated her to stand. Thankfully, the mist had lifted so the trees were in clear view. She rubbed her head and stumbled toward the far part of the woods.

Mary awoke a short time later with the same pounding in her head. Moaning, she squeezed her eyes shut and pushed on her temples. "Did Humberly put any medicine in our satchels?"

Receiving no answer, she reluctantly opened her eyes and was surprised to see Charlotte gone. She looked all around and instead of concern, felt a rush of anger boil up inside. "She left me here? How could she?!"

At first, Mary was startled by the negative thoughts going through her mind. Any worry on behalf of her friend seemed to be missing and was replaced with unfamiliar feelings of irritability and resentment. But the more she allowed her thoughts to consume her, the better it felt directing her moodiness at someone. When she realized how thirsty she was, her grumblings about Charlotte only grew worse.

"If I leave to get a drink, Charlotte won't know where to find me. Then I'll be to blame, even though she left me here in the first place. She can be so selfish sometimes. I would never do that to her!"

Deep inside, a twinge of conviction revealed the truth of the situation, but it was easier to listen to the lie in her sour mood. As time passed, her misery only grew, fueling the negativity she was experiencing. She paced back and forth, complaining aloud about Charlotte's thoughtlessness. Certainly, she had left her there on purpose and was now back at the tavern laughing at her. Mary's overwhelming thoughts distracted her from seeing the glowing brooch on her cloak.

She scanned the landscape after deciding to look for water after all, when a dark figure stepped out from behind the tree. Mary jumped, startled that someone was listening to her tirade. "Sorry, I didn't know anyone else was here."

She tried to hide her uneasiness that she wasn't alone. As the figure came into full view, there was something strangely familiar about him. He removed his hood, revealing an unusually pale face with a large scar down his right cheek. Now Mary knew where she had seen him. He was the man at the Tavern- the one who kept staring at her.

Despite the many reasons she had to feel frightened of him, she was mostly taken aback by the intensity of his glare. "Forgive me for frightening you, dear." His voice was a hoarse whisper. "I try to avoid the light."

"That's alright." She could tell she sounded calmer than she felt. "I guess it is pretty bright out." The gray clouds were now completely blocking the sun. "Sort of."

The man continued. "I couldn't help but overhear how selfish your friend was in leaving you here all alone." Mary bristled at the reminder that she was by herself with this strange man. "If I were you," he continued, "I'd choose my companions more carefully."

He came nearer and pulled a piece of fruit from the tree. "Care for another?" It was obvious to Mary that he was trying to sound sweet, but his voice came across rather sickly.

His bony outstretched hand held the fruit as he forced a smile. Even though it appeared harmless, she now knew the poison it held inside. She turned her face away in refusal saying, "I already had some, thanks."

The man's mouth turned upward as he let the piece fall to the ground. Mary watched it roll down the small hill, not wanting to meet his gaze. "Of course. My associates will be thrilled to learn that a royal heir has tried our delightful fruit."

"Wait, how do you know I'm an heir?" She looked up, but the man had once again disappeared. "How does he keep doing that?!" But she was relieved that he was no longer there. The tree trunk offered some stability while his last words made her thoughts run wild.

After a few minutes, the grass near her feet began to shift. Suddenly, a small head crept up making her jump. "Ssoo, you're the royal heir, hmm?" The red and black snake slithered closer. She stood against the tree, too frightened to move. "Don't worry. I'm not here to harm you," he hissed.

"What do you want?"

"Jusst to chat." The snake slowly coiled itself in the grass. "I hear you're the one desstined to overthrow the great darkness."

"I, I don't know," she stammered. Once more, she was beginning to feel unsure about everything. The snake hissed again.

"Only ssomeone with great power can overthrow thiss darkness. Only ssomeone of true royal blood."

"Well... I *am* an heir."

The snake rubbed his scales together making a coarse, raspy sound. "You may be an heir," he said inching closer, "but you're merely a little girl. A very sscared little girl. What makess you think you're sso powerful?"

"I'm not. Not really. My dad should be the one here, but he won't come." She said this more to herself than to the snake.

"Ahh, sso your father iss the *true* heir. *He* should be the one wearing the crown."

Mary wanted to object, but she felt what the snake was saying was true. Her dad could do a far better job ruling than she could. *How could anyone expect me to run a kingdom when I'm not even old enough to drive?*

"Perhapss, you're better off in your own world. With ssomeone more... legitimate... taking the crown."

Mary could feel her defenses weakening. She already had her doubts, but now she felt completely disheartened.

Why did I think I could do this? she thought. *I don't have any right to rule this land. I only came here because Charlotte made me, and now even she's gone. Some friend she is. Maybe I should just go home.* Knowing from her silence that he had done his job, the snake slithered away.

Charlotte had finally found a stream and was just dipping her hands in for a drink. She closed her eyes and splashed her face with water unaware of the man in the black cloak watching from a distance. When she sat up, a large snake was coiled beside her, making her gasp and fall backward.

"Don't be afraid. I mean you no harm," he said, enjoying her reaction.

Seeing the snake's markings, she relaxed. "You *only* startled me. You're not even venomous."

The snake hissed violently, but Charlotte had never been afraid of snakes before and was not about to start now. She took one more drink and began walking back to the tree. He quickly slithered to catch up.

"I wass jusst with your friend. Mary."

"Oh yeah?" She was getting increasingly annoyed with the unwelcome visitor.

"She had ssomething very interessting to ssay."

Charlotte glanced at the snake but didn't respond.

"She ssaid that when she becomess queen she planss to make you her sservant."

Charlotte stopped. Even though deep down she knew it wasn't true, she couldn't help feeling angry. "Mary wouldn't do that," she said. Her jaw clenched tightly though, as the sense of betrayal rose. "And even if she did say it, she can forget it. I'm the one who found the map. She wouldn't even be here if it wasn't for me dragging her along. If anything, I deserve to be the royal heir. I'm just as important as she is." The snake crept along, sensing he had struck a nerve.

"It ssoundss as if you're jealouss."

"I am not jealous!"

"Of coursse you are. Every girl wantss to be a princesss."

Charlotte couldn't tell if she was angrier at the snake or Mary. "Maybe you should jusst *take* the crown. You'd be a far better queen than her anyway." Charlotte's eyebrows furrowed.

"Maybe I will. I'm just as special as she is."

"Of coursse you are," the snake coaxed.

"And then I'll make her *my* servant." She looked victoriously at the snake. He smiled back, aware of his success, before slithering out into the woods. Quickly dismissing his departure, she was determined to tell Mary what she thought.

When Charlotte emerged from the woods, Mary was hastily pacing in front of the tree. Soon, she glanced up and began angrily walking toward Charlotte. As soon as Charlotte was within earshot she began to shout.

"Where have you been? I've been waiting forever for you!"

"I've only been gone 20 minutes!"

"Well, you shouldn't have left me in the first place!"

Charlotte felt a pang of guilt, but she pushed it aside to make her point. "Why should I care? You just want to make me your servant!"

Mary's mouth dropped open in surprise.

"That's right! I know what you said. Do you think you can use me to get the crown and then just push me aside? Maybe I'll just take the crown for myself! What would you do then, huh?"

Mary was still too stunned to speak. Suddenly, tears filled her eyes. "Maybe you should," she cried. Charlotte hadn't expected Mary to agree with her. She wasn't sure how to respond. "I don't deserve the crown. I don't even want to be an heir. I just want to go home." She sat down in the grass and continued to sob.

It was clear the snake had fooled Charlotte. Mary obviously had no intention of making Charlotte her servant. *Why had I believed that reptile anyway?* Her face grew warm with shame. Finding a spot to sit, she put her arm around her friend. "I'm sorry. I didn't mean what I said. There was this snake, and he said some things that made me upset and…"

"You saw a snake, too?"

"Yeah. He said he had already talked to you."

At that moment, Humberly appeared from the woods. "There you are!" he said sharply. "I specifically told you *not* to go to the northern side of the village."

The girls looked around. "We're sorry, Humberly," Charlotte answered. "We didn't realize we had wandered so far."

He sighed. "I should've known you'd follow the butterflies." One of the returning creatures fluttered from his shoulder as he brushed it aside.

When he noticed Mary's tears, his tone shifted. "What happened here?"

Charlotte felt sheepish. "I said some things I shouldn't have."

"It's not your fault," Mary interrupted. "I shouldn't even be here."

He studied the girls for a moment. "This is what I feared."

"What?" Charlotte asked.

"The Tree of Deception. It is the exact reason I didn't want you coming here alone."

Charlotte followed Humberly's gaze. "The fruit tasted so good, but it gave us the worst stomach aches."

"Sweet on the tongue, sour in the stomach. Sometimes the worst things for us look the most appealing. Did you notice how your thoughts shifted after you ate the fruit?"

Mary and Charlotte pondered for a moment. "I did wake up in a horrible mood, and I couldn't stop blaming Charlotte for everything."

He nodded. "It's a very subtle toxin. It stirs up distrust and fear. Which is why you must cling to the truth even when it doesn't *feel* true."

He pulled a few items from his satchel and began crushing them together in a cup. He mixed in a liquid and handed it to Mary.

"What is it? It smells awful."

"It's called Rethorian, derived from the Tree of Authenticity. It makes the toxins of the fruit wear off faster."

"I'll drink anything if it makes this go away," Mary responded. She held her nose, took a long sip, then handed the mixture to Charlotte. After a few minutes, she could feel her mood lifting. She no longer felt misplaced and insignificant. In fact, as the solution took its full effect, she became more determined than ever to fulfill her calling.

Charlotte noticed the look in Mary's eyes. Whatever the Tree of Deception had persuaded her of, the Tree of Authenticity had cured and revived. Even in herself, the insecurity diminished and her sense of worth was strengthened.

Mary reached over and hugged Charlotte tightly. "I would never make you my servant."

"I know," she admitted. "I'm too messy."

The girls laughed as they stood to their feet.

"That's better," Humberly remarked, packing his bag. "With the storm having passed, we may be able to get something done after all." He nodded toward the tree. "Hopefully, something good will come out of it by the day's end."

"A gem is hidden in the tree?" Charlotte asked with surprise.

"Don't worry, it can't do you any more harm." He slung his satchel over his shoulder and caught a glimpse of the new brooch on Mary's cloak. "Did you purchase that in town?"

"Mm-hmm. Well, Annabel gave it to me when we stopped in her store. She gave Charlotte perfume too."

His brow creased. "You say Annabel gave it to you?"

"Why do you look so worried?"

He shrugged his shoulders. "I've never met her personally, but I've heard rumors she's one of the king's followers. I would be mindful if I were you. She may not be trustworthy."

"She was pretty odd," Charlotte admitted. "And she knew of us even before we met."

"She's just different," Mary reasoned. "And she said someone told her our names."

Charlotte and Humberly looked skeptical, but Mary wasn't ready to believe Annabel was the enemy. Not after she'd been so kind to them. Ignoring Humberly's concern, she wiped a smudge off of her brooch and straightened it affectionately.

Humberly led the girls back to the tree and placed his paw against the bark, examining its branches.

"The inhabitants of Ilyor might admire this tree for its appearance, but they would never partake of its fruit. For reasons you girls have already discovered. This is why the fruit is the most likely place for the gem to be hidden."

Charlotte looked at the now unappealing fruit. "But if it was hidden so long ago, wouldn't all of the old fruit have rotted away by now and new fruit have grown?"

"The fruit in Ilyor never rots. It merely waits to be chosen." He studied the fruit closest to him. "It does seem rather impossible to tell which one is the vessel. Unfortunately, we may have to cut them all open."

"But there are so many," Mary said. "It will take until after dark."

"Yes," he replied thoughtfully, rubbing his chin. "Unless..." He took Mary's hand, leading her toward the tree. "If this gem glows as strongly as the others, we should be able to see it through the fruit's skin."

"It's worth a try," Mary said in agreement. The others stared intently as she cradled each piece in her hand, slowly making her way around the tree.

Chapter Twelve

Aid in Strange Places

A s piece after piece revealed nothing, Charlotte lay down in the grass, rubbing her shoulders. The strain in her neck from looking up was beginning to make her doubt the gem was anywhere nearby. Closing her eyes, she let her body sink into the cool grass. The sun occasionally broke through the clouds to warm her skin and made all the worries of the day fade away.

It was a long while before she opened her eyes again. When she did, she was happy with what she saw. The gray clouds had finally passed and the tree glistened as the remaining rain droplets sparkled in the sun. She realized from this angle that most of the tree was visible at once. Maybe this was the best way to search after all.

Starting from the bottom and studying one limb at a time, it was difficult to determine if any fruit in particular looked unusual. Some were a bit plumper than others, but overall, they were generally the same size and color.

Not helpful.

The middle section held more of the same until finally, close to the top, a piece stood out from the rest. Getting up to examine it more closely, she found it was more pear-shaped than the others, with a long, brown mark down its side resembling a scar. A wave of excitement swept over her. The mark must be where the gem was inserted.

"Over here!" she called.

Mary didn't want to lose her place, but her arms and back ached so badly that the welcome distraction offered some relief. They all hoped Charlotte had put an end to their search. As she pointed out the strange curve of the fruit and the "scar" down its side, it seemed undeniable that it was the one.

Now they just had to get it. Mary stood by the trunk, intending to lift Charlotte, but Charlotte didn't move. The thought of her last climb was still fresh in her mind. "Maybe someone else can get this one," she said.

"Unfortunately, I'm unable to climb trees," Humberly said.

Charlotte looked at him in surprise. "But how do you get the key from the enchanted tree?"

"There are other ways. Plus, I don't believe this tree is enchanted in the same way." He said this to calm her fears of being surprised again.

She already knew Mary's fear of heights would keep the fruit far from her reach. So, saying a short prayer under her breath, she reluctantly walked toward the trunk. *Might as well get this over with now.* The fear certainly wasn't going to keep her from climbing forever.

Setting her foot in Mary's hand, the first branch felt thick and strong. It was also much lower than the enchanted tree and easier to climb. Feeling steady enough, she climbed to another branch, then another. She focused only on the goal, not letting any other thoughts press in.

When she took hold of the fruit, the scar felt rough on her fingertips. The piece was also firmer than she expected as though it hadn't quite ripened yet. She bent the stem back and forth until it finally broke free, and dropped it into the waiting hands below.

It wasn't until her feet were firmly on the ground again that she realized just how nervous she'd been. Climbing trees in this world was *not* as enjoyable.

They all held their breath while the fruit sat in Mary's open hand. If there was a gem glowing inside, it was impossible to tell at this point. Just to be certain, Humberly cut the fruit open. The purple liquid flowed out from the clear flesh within. Disappointed, he let it fall to the ground. "Let's keep looking."

"Wait," Mary said, touching his arm. She pointed to a small fruit hanging behind where the other had been. It was surprising how much smaller it was than the rest like it hadn't finished growing. She doubted this would be the hiding place of such a valuable gem, but it didn't hurt to try—as long as Charlotte was willing to climb again.

Charlotte knew the question that was coming. She placed her hand on Mary's shoulder, steadying herself for another boost. Climbing felt easier this time, especially since she knew she wouldn't be catapulted into the air.

This new piece of fruit felt different. It was much softer than the rest and was a deeper shade of purple. As soon as Mary caught the fruit, the color of the peel began to soften from purple to pink. She wrapped her fingers around it feeling its warmth. Soon, the color changed so drastically, it was as if the fruit wasn't there at all.

Reluctantly, Mary handed it to Humberly so that he could cut it in half. There, instead of a pit, was a radiant amethyst jewel. Charlotte squealed in delight and squeezed Mary's hand.

"That makes three," Humberly said happily, slipping the gem into his satchel. "This day proved to be productive after all. We're now free to rest for the evening."

They all walked cheerfully toward the woods. It was around two o'clock and the girls were glad they'd be able to relax after the turmoil of the afternoon. Then a thought occurred to Mary.

"Humberly, do you remember the man I saw at the tavern?"

"You mean the one only you could see?" He said smiling softly.

"Yeah, that one. He was here again. He came by after I woke up and talked to me before the snake came."

He stopped. "A snake? What color was it?"

Charlotte chimed in. "He was red, black, and annoying. He's the one who put the awful ideas in our heads."

Mary nodded. "Also, the man said his companions would be glad to hear that an heir had tried their fruit. How did he know that I'm an heir?"

Humberly's face became grave. "I'm afraid we won't have time to rest, after all, girls."

Charlotte stifled a groan.

"It seems word has gotten out about our plan. I believe the man you saw was Delirion, the king's chief advisor. I'm sorry I didn't believe you earlier, Mary. He's very powerful and very dangerous. The king must know we're coming for the crown."

"What do we do?" Mary asked, a twinge of panic in her voice.

"We'll pick up our things in the village and go to the next location on the map. With any luck, we'll stay one step ahead of Delirion."

The trio hurried toward the village and stopped briefly at the tavern. After saying a quick goodbye to Maribel, Humberly led them northward toward the mines. He set a swift pace, stopping only to check the map periodically.

Even though there was little time to rest, the pleasantness of the forest didn't escape them. The birds chirped happily in the trees while rabbits and squirrels bustled up and down the path, unaware of the critical journey unfolding before them.

When evening settled on the forest, the creatures disappeared into their homes, one by one. By this point, it had been several hours since they'd started walking, and it seemed as though the forest would never end. Charlotte held the magical perfume ready to test its performance by making Humberly stop and take a break. Mary seemed to read her thoughts though and gave her a nudge. Charlotte reluctantly put the bottle away.

Instead, she thought one of Humberly's stories might help pass the time. "Humberly, how did you meet Mary's uncle?" she asked. It seemed Humberly stood a bit straighter at the mention of Uncle Richard.

He turned his head slightly with a half-smile. "It was a little while after I'd begun searching for the gems. On my way home one day, I found Sir Richard halfway up a tree trying to ward off a very angry badger. I guess he'd accidentally crushed one of its tunnels and the animal was set to tear him to pieces. I think Sir Richard was less afraid of the badger's teeth though, than he was of the fact that the animal could *talk*. He was absolutely beside himself when the badger began yelling at him. He'd just come to this world and still wasn't familiar with all of its *peculiarities*." He chuckled.

"Did you save him?" Mary asked.

"I suppose so. I tried to reason with the badger first, of course, but he quickly turned on me too. As I recall, he was snarling at me for siding with an outsider. Not everyone here is as welcoming to visitors, you know. It was obvious that one of us would end up with a new scar if I didn't do something soon. So, I used a little Powder of Paralysis to make our escape."

"You mean you paralyzed the badger?" Mary asked.

"Only for a few minutes," he assured her. "Long enough for us to get away."

"Why didn't we use *that* on the serpent?" Charlotte asked in surprise.

"It's extremely hard to come by. I happened to have a little left from another expedition.

"Anyway, your uncle was very grateful and showed a lot of interest in the powder. We got to talking, which took a little getting used to on his part, and the rest is history."

Charlotte and Mary enjoyed the amusing story of Uncle Richard's first time hearing a talking animal. They could easily relate to the surprise and smiled remembering their reactions to meeting Humberly.

After a while, when Mary began rethinking her decision about the perfume, the trees finally opened, revealing a large babbling brook running through a grassy field.

"We've made good time," Humberly noted. "We can stop for dinner."

The girls breathed a sigh of relief as they set down their things. "Mary, why don't you set up a picnic while Charlotte and I gather some berries? I believe there are some over that hill."

Leaving Mary near the water, he guided Charlotte across the field to some leafy bushes. After a quick inspection, he instructed her to watch closely. Moving the leaves aside, he touched a closed blossom. Its petals instantly opened up to reveal a tiny red ball in the center. Twisting the ball, he plucked it off and popped it into his mouth.

"Autumn berries are some of the sweetest in Ilyor. Give it a try."

Charlotte reached for a flower and grinned as its petals extended. Following his example, she took the berry and twisted. But rather than popping off, it was crushed between her fingers.

"Firm, but gentle."

After a few tries, she finally got the hang of it and excitedly put the berry in her mouth. Her eyes grew wide as she chewed the delicious fruit. It tasted like sweet grapes and peaches despite being a berry.

"How does everything in Ilyor taste so good?"

Humberly smiled. The two set out to fill their pouches, enjoying the peaceful setting. Charlotte couldn't help but eat more berries than she collected.

After a short while, she finally broke the silence. "Humberly, can I ask you a question?"

"Of course, dear."

"It feels silly to ask this, but... do you think I'm important? You know, like Mary?"

He stopped picking for a moment to look at her. Her red hair wrapped around her face as a light breeze picked up.

"Why would you ask such a question?" he said kindly.

"Well," she hesitated, "it's just that Mary is royalty now, and I'm just... well, I'm still plain old Charlotte."

He chuckled. "Plain old Charlotte, huh?"

"Yeah. I mean, I'm not going to be running a whole kingdom or anything. So, there's nothing that really makes me special."

Humberly was quiet for a moment before responding. When he did, his tone was serious. "It's my turn to ask you a question... Who convinced Mary to come on this journey?"

She shrugged. "Mary wanted to come, she was just nervous."

"Hmm. And who climbed the tree and found the secret cottage?"

"I did. But only because Mary told me to."

"And who distracted the deadly serpent?"

"Well, we had to help Mary get the gem."

"Yes, exactly. You and Mary are a good team. I don't think she would become what she is meant to be without your friendship. Nothing will change that—not even her royal status. Who you *are* is what makes you special, Charlotte, not your title. And you'll need one another now more than ever."

Charlotte stopped picking berries. After a moment, she looked up. "I guess Mary and I are both special in our own way, whether we're royalty or not." He returned her smile with a small nod. *Maybe the same is true for my new sister too,* she thought.

Once their pouches were full, the pair began walking back across the field. Suddenly, they came across a strange little man. "Come! Come with me!" He spoke in a shrill voice. "We have your friend. Your friend, Mary."

Charlotte gasped. "Where is she?!" Without waiting for an answer, she dropped the berries and began to run.

Chapter Thirteen

Drollmin

While Charlotte and Humberly were picking berries, Mary laid out the food Maribel insisted they bring. It was late in the evening, and the trees cast long shadows along the brook. The deep green grass was so soft, it was like sitting on a feather bed. She was sure there wasn't a more beautiful place in any land.

While she waited, she strolled along the water's edge. Colorful pebbles lined the bottom of the stream while weeping willows skimmed its surface. The water was crystal clear.

The steady rhythm of a small waterfall helped her unwind as she slipped off her boots and waded into the stream. The cool water soothed her weary legs. A yellow fish darted around her, and schools of red minnows swam between her legs.

Hopping along the flat stones, she landed next to the waterfall and ran her fingers through its flow, unable to resist scooping some into her mouth. It had a subtle sweetness, urging her to drink until her stomach gurgled.

She stood for some time, watching the water cascade over the rock and disappear below. The glistening torrent was enticing and just tall enough for her to stand underneath if she wanted. She suddenly had an irresistible urge to lean forward. As she pressed in, her foot slipped from the rock she was standing on causing her to lose her balance.

With a loud squeal, she went tumbling through the water, catching herself on the cold stone floor. "Ow!" A throb of pain shot through her hands and knees.

The small amount of light shining through the cascade revealed narrow stone walls leading up to a low ceiling. Slowly, she recovered her footing to examine her freshly scraped knee.

"Most people just walk through, you know."

Mary jumped at the strange voice, smacking her head on the ceiling. She winced, rubbing her latest injury.

A small man in a dark blue robe stepped into the light.

"Who are you?" she asked.

"I didn't mean to startle you. My name is Pickney, leader of the Drollmin. I'm sorry our entrance isn't more accommodating. You're a bit bigger than our usual guests."

"Oh, no, it's fine," she replied with uncertainty. "You live in this cave?"

"Why, of course. Despite how it seems, it's quite spacious once you're inside. I do hope you'll join us; we've just heated up molasses and tea."

While he was talking, she took the opportunity to examine him more closely. He couldn't have been more than four feet tall. His long, white beard came down to his knees, and his wispy white hair stuck out in all directions, almost as if he'd recently been electrocuted. She glanced back to see if she could spot Charlotte and Humberly.

"Your friends will come along shortly," Pickney said. "In the meantime, you're safe with us." He smiled warmly and then turned to the back of the cave. Mary wasn't sure what she should do, but she found herself following him anyway.

As they walked along the winding tunnel, she could feel the air getting cooler.

We must be going farther underground, she thought. Finally, a soft light emerged. As her eyes adjusted, she saw precious stones strewn along the tunnel floor. It was a beautiful contrast to the surrounding soil. Pickney hurried on ahead of her, glancing back every so often to be sure she was keeping up.

Soon, she heard the dull hum of voices in the near distance. "They'll be thrilled to meet you," he remarked with a peculiar laugh.

Mary chewed her bottom lip wondering what she had gotten herself into. *Why would these strangers want to meet me? Pickney seems harmless enough, but what if these other people aren't? Maybe I shouldn't have come down here alone.*

As the noise became louder, her stomach grew tighter. She wanted to turn and run, but before she had the nerve, he took her arm, pulling her into a brightly lit cavern filled with dozens of small men.

Immediately, the noise stopped as every eye focused on her. She shifted uneasily with her arm still clasped in Pickney's firm grip. He didn't say anything at first because there was no need. His face told them everything they needed to know.

Suddenly, a roar filled the cavern. The men beat the tables with their fists and hollered in a strange language. It was so loud, it was hard to tell if they were excited or furious.

When she looked to Pickney for answers she found he was wildly waving his free arm and howling along with them. Humberly had better find her, and fast. She thought about running back the way she came, but Pickney still had her arm in his strong grip.

Eventually, he motioned for silence and the men returned to their seats. He stood beside her, raising his voice as he addressed the room. "My friends, we have been waiting a long time for this moment. Some of us were beginning to doubt it would ever come. But the struggle against this darkness is finally coming to an end. At long last, we have found the one who will change our future."

Mary felt her face grow red as she realized this bold statement was directed at her. At least they seemed to have no intention of hurting her. When the resumed shouting slowly died down, Pickney turned to her.

"As you can see, we are all very excited you've arrived. We've been waiting quite some time to find the one who will restore the crown."

"But how do you know who I am?"

"We didn't. At least not until the sacred gem began to glow. Since it's never done that before, we assumed something had to be causing it. When I went to find out what it could be, you stumbled through. I figured I had my answer." The Drollmin chuckled. "Now, right this way."

He led her to the back of the cavern. Feeling only mildly unsure now, she quickly took in her surroundings. The cavern was surprisingly large with minimal furnishings. The floor and walls were covered in intricate patterns of colorful stones. Small mahogany tables lined the walls, with multiple tunnels leading away from the main hollow. Ice crystals hanging from the ceiling shone in all different shades of yellows, reds, and oranges. The light reflecting off of the colorful jewels created a stunning effect.

"We discovered the gem a few decades ago," he stated, recapturing her attention, "and we've been hiding it here ever since." He pointed to the far wall where the glowing emerald was embedded in the surface.

Mary gasped at the discovery of the fourth gem. Even though it was out of reach, she could feel its warmth drawing her near. "But I thought the last gem was hidden in the mines," she said, forcing herself to focus on his response.

"Indeed. And it was no easy task retrieving it, mind you. It was being heavily guarded by numerous gremlins."

"How did you know where to look?"

"We didn't, but as you may have noticed, we Drollmin are very fond of digging. Since being above ground has become too dangerous, it's given us a way to travel without anyone noticing." He gestured to the various tunnels.

"We were digging up north one day when we discovered an underground cavern. After we broke through the wall, a horde of gremlins rushed toward us screeching in their garbled language. They began attacking us with swords and spears, so naturally, we fought back. Our digging tools came in handy and we battled long and hard until the last gremlin was overcome."

A chill went through Mary. She was grateful the Drollmin had already fought for this gem.

"Now, it's rare to find gremlins underground due to their poor eyesight," he continued, "and because there were so many, we knew they were there for a reason. We searched the room and found a small iron chest hidden in the corner which held this extraordinary stone.

"Of course, it wasn't glowing like it is now, but we Drollmin know a precious stone when we see it." He widened his eyes to elaborate his point.

"We replaced the gem with one of similar size and color and then dosed our enemies with a memory potion so they would forget our encounter. Being gremlins, I doubt they ever knew the difference." He laughed at his cleverness. "Now, many years later, here we are."

Mary was amazed by the Drollmin's story. She was also grateful to have such brave men fighting on her side.

Without warning, one of the Drollmin brought Humberly and Charlotte into the cave.

"Mary!" Charlotte tried to hide the worry in her voice. "I'm so glad you're okay! How did you get here?"

She hugged Charlotte. "I fell through the waterfall."

Charlotte looked down at her own soggy clothes. "They should make a dryer entrance." The gem glowed brightly beyond Mary's shoulder. "Is that the last gem?!"

"Yes. The Drollmin found it in the mines."

Humberly came forward to shake Pickney's hand. "You've done well, my friend. This will cut off a large portion of our journey. And with the henchmen going to the mines, we'll have a chance to rest for the night."

"Excellent! We'll all celebrate. There are better days to come!"

All the men cheered and the trio couldn't help but join in. The crown finally seemed within reach.

Pickney left to begin preparations while an older Drollmin handed the guests dry clothes and led them to their rooms. The girls' bedroom was slightly larger than Humberly's, with two wooden beds, matching side tables, and a small fireplace. Gems sparkled on the ceiling and walls, and a braided rug covered the floor.

"Hang your clothes by the fire to dry," the man advised before leaving.

Doing as he said, they changed quickly and stood by the fire to escape the chill. By this time, they were getting hungry. "We should have brought our picnic," Mary stated when Humberly rejoined them.

"Already taken care of—along with your boots." Mary was given the boots to put back on.

While he went to retrieve the basket from one of the Drollmin, the girls made themselves comfortable at a long table. Upon returning, he spread the contents out before them. Even though they had more than enough for the three of them, Drollmin kept walking by, piling more food onto their table.

"They sure know how to eat around here," Charlotte commented, retrieving one of the elaborate goblets of punch being handed out.

Each of the men came by to toast their new friends, leaving behind a smooth round object that resembled a small stone. After the third one, Charlotte and Mary questioned Humberly.

"It's tradition. You'll understand soon enough." After trying to pry it open, squeeze it, and make it bounce, they finally set them aside, resigned to wait for the demonstration.

Once everyone had their fill, a youngling took out the fiddle and began to play. Others joined him and the cavern was filled with a lively tune. Many stomped their feet and sang with fervor. Most of the songs were in the Drollmin's language, so the girls just clapped along happily. The party was soon in full swing.

A large fire was lit in the middle of the dirt floor, and the men who were singing began dancing around it, throwing the small stone-like objects into the blaze. Every time this happened, the flames ignited in an explosion of color. The crowd would cheer and the music would play even faster.

Mary and Charlotte gasped in fascination. "Put a few in your pocket," Humberly suggested with a twinkle in his eye. When Pickney and another Drollmin scooped the girls up to dance, they willingly joined in, excited to try this unfamiliar custom.

As they moved around the flames, they took turns tossing in pellets and watching the flames erupt. With each new flare, the music would quicken, until soon they were keeping pace at a dizzying speed.

Charlotte and Mary moved their legs as fast as they could, trying their best to keep up with the lively footwork. When the song finally ended, they collapsed onto the nearby benches, laughing breathlessly.

Their break didn't last long, however. When the music began again, they were instantly pulled to their feet. Despite being almost a foot shorter, the men swept them along, impressively leading them around the floor. Dance after dance, the girls were kept in motion.

Finally, when it felt as if their legs would give way, they fell onto the bench beside Humberly. With bright eyes and broad smiles, they sat, catching their breath. Emptying her goblet, Charlotte raised it in the air to request another.

Just then, Mary's broach began to glow. Charlotte eyed it suspiciously. "Isn't that supposed to warn you of danger?" Looking down, Mary slanted it toward her face.

"That's strange." She looked around, wondering what it could mean. "Maybe it's broken," she finally decided and let it fall back into place. After a minute the glowing stopped.

Humberly, who had joined in the dancing for a time, was now nose-deep in the map. "Where to next?" Mary asked, shifting the conversation.

He looked up as if he'd forgotten anyone was there. "Oh, hmm-mm. It appears the "X" is in the northwestern part of the kingdom." He laid it down on the table, pointing to the farthest corner. "With the terrain, it will take at least a few days to get there."

"Isn't there a faster way?" Charlotte asked.

"Not that I can see. All paths to the castle have been cut off for quite some time."

At that point, Pickney arrived to refill his guests' glasses. "Why so glum? This is a celebration."

"Don't worry, we're still enjoying ourselves," Humberly assured him. "We're simply going over tomorrow's plans. It seems we'll have our work cut out for us."

Pickney peered over his shoulder. "Well, I'll say. It looks as though you have to scale old Crescent." He set his jug down on the table. "There are easier ways to travel through the kingdom, you know." He looked at the girls with a twinkle in his eye.

Humberly raised his eyebrow.

"I'm referring to the tunnels, of course," he explained." They can take you wherever you want to go without anyone spotting you."

"Even to the western kingdom?" Humberly looked skeptical.

"The west, the east, the north, and south. They only stop short of the king's land itself."

Humberly brightened. "Well, isn't that something? That will save us a few hard day's journey, girls."

They both smiled. "Does that mean we can stay up later tonight?" Charlotte asked.

"We still need our rest. But you can enjoy the party a little while longer."

Mary and Charlotte continued to dance until their sides ached from laughter. When Humberly motioned them over, they were both ready to tumble into bed. Saying goodnight to the Drollmin, and thanking them for the party, they went to their room.

After changing into thermals, Charlotte crawled under the covers and discovered her feet hanging over the edge. She glanced at Mary's wiggling toes. "I feel like a giant," she said giggling. Blowing out the lit candle, she curled up her legs and nestled into the warm bed.

"I don't think I've ever had so much fun," Mary whispered. Charlotte agreed, thinking how the songs seemed to lift her off her feet.

The music in the main cavern had softened and was now playing a quiet melody. Unable to stay awake any longer, they drifted off to sleep, imagining themselves gliding to the music.

Chapter Fourteen

The Bowmik

The next morning, Humberly came in early, stirring the girls from their sleep. "Rise and shine. It's a long journey ahead."

"Five more minutes," Charlotte said with a moan.

"Not today. There's no time to waste."

They slowly pulled back the covers. "It's so dark. Is it even morning yet?" Mary asked through a big yawn.

"The sun will be up shortly. Not that we will know, however, being in a cave of course. Once we eat, we'll be on our way."

Dragging themselves out of bed, the girls rubbed the sleep from their eyes. Their clothes were warm from hanging by the fire, and they joined the others in the main cavern once they dressed.

After the cozy beds, the benches at the tables felt much harder than they had the night before. Charlotte squirmed in place trying to get comfortable. Humberly served two plates from the steaming pot on the table. He set a simple breakfast of ham and grits in front of them.

"It's too early for breakfast," Charlotte murmured. But Mary, who was a morning person, was wide awake at this point.

"You should be excited. We're searching for the crown today!"

Charlotte smirked. "I'll be excited if it comes on a feather bed."

Mary smiled and took a bite of her grits. "I don't think we'll be that lucky."

After eating, Pickney offered to guide them to the end of the tunnel. "It won't get you as far as you need, but it will bring you well under the mountain."

"Which will be sufficient," Humberly assured him.

As their visitors prepared to leave, the Drollmin eagerly shook their hands, wishing them well. The three said goodbyes, thanking their gracious hosts, and exited down a dimly lit tunnel. Pickney led the way, holding a large torch, of which smaller styles hung every few yards. After walking for a time, Mary stopped short.

"The gem!" she cried, eyes wide with concern. "It's still back in the cavern!"

Charlotte let out a soft moan.

"Don't worry," Humberly replied calmly. Pickney gave it to me this morning." He gently patted his satchel.

Relief swept over the girls. "If we had to go back, I might have used my perfume to make you carry me," Charlotte said with a grin.

They continued to travel on relatively flat ground for over an hour, being sure to follow Pickney around every twist and turn. Even with minimal lighting, they could easily find their footing, excluding the occasional bulging root.

Aware of the long journey ahead, Pickney did his best to lead them on the most level paths, knowing it wouldn't remain that way for long. Rounding the last even bend, they faced what appeared to be a stone wall. "A dead end?" Charlotte asked.

Pickney shook his head. "Here's where our tools come in handy." He took two pickaxes from his bag and began to climb, grasping the rough stone with his rubber-soled boots. Moving closer, the group could see the tunnel didn't end but rose in a sharp incline.

"I hope we don't have to do that," Mary stated.

When he reached the top, he tied a long rope to a fixed boulder and threw the other end down. "Use the wall to help you."

The girls looked at Humberly. "I guess I'll go first," he said. Taking the rope in his hands, he secured his feet and slowly moved up the slope while leaning back for better support.

They watched his tail follow him as he swiftly scaled the wall. When he made it to the top, he tightened the line and instructed them to go one at a time. Grasping it firmly, Charlotte tugged to see if the rope would hold. "I hope this is easier than in gym class." Putting one foot in a crevice, she pulled herself up and tried to remain steady. Without enough grip, however, she quickly lost her footing.

"Keep your feet planted in front of you and shift your weight back," Humberly advised.

She tried again. After a few more failed attempts, she finally began to understand the balance. Leaning as far back as she dared, and keeping her feet in view, she slowly made her way up the slope, reaching the top with a wide grin. "Well done," Humberly praised, checking the rope again. "You're up," he yelled down.

Achieving a firm grip, Mary kept her eyes forward. She wasn't as coordinated as Charlotte, but learning from her missteps gave her a better idea of where to start. It was strange at first to lean back so far, but she soon grew more comfortable with it, and it wasn't long before she was maneuvering up the incline toward the others. Humberly patted her on the back while Pickney untied the rope.

"Did you make the path that way just for fun?" Charlotte teased.

"Normally we wouldn't have," he answered, missing the joke, "but we hit the largest diamond we'd ever seen and couldn't get around it. We weren't working with diamond-tipped drills at the time. I'm afraid the rest of the way isn't much better."

She and Mary exchanged looks. "Of course, there are diamonds the size of boulders here," Charlotte said and almost laughed.

The next few miles proved to be as challenging as he said. The path became cramped and jagged, with very little level ground. While some portions sloped downward, others forced them to climb again, clinging to rocks and crevices. One section was so narrow, they had to crawl on their hands and knees to get through. By the time they stopped, they were worn out and covered in dirt.

Pickney poured water over their faces and hands.

"We made it through the hardest stretch," he said encouragingly. "Not much farther now." He handed each of them some dried fruit and jerky. "We'll rest only a few minutes before moving on."

The girls found he wasn't kidding when he said a few minutes. When he picked up his bag again, they felt they'd only just sat down. Struggling to their feet, they stretched and rubbed their sore muscles before following the others.

Fortunately, as Pickney suggested, the path gradually became smoother. There weren't any more boulders to scale, and the only hindrance was a stubbed toe from the occasional rock. Even though they were still making progress, the calmer pace helped them recuperate more quickly.

Soon, Pickney was whistling a familiar tune. Recognizing it from the night before, the girls joined in where they could as Humberly sang along. The music lifted their spirits and helped pass the time. After another mile or two, he came to a stop. It seemed to the others that they had hit another dead end. "This is where I leave you."

Dragging a ladder out of nowhere, he leaned it against the far wall and climbed to the top. The girls breathed a sigh of relief. Even though they enjoyed the Drollmin's company, they were eager to escape the tunnels and breathe fresh air.

He unhooked a small latch and cautiously peered out. After several moments, he returned to give the all-clear.

Humberly was the first to step forward. "Thank you for all you've done, Pickney. We couldn't have done this without you."

"You're most welcome. If you need access to the tunnels again, call on Redwin. He guards the west entrance."

Humberly nodded before shaking his hand and climbing the ladder.

"I hope we see you again soon," Charlotte said, giving him a warm hug.

"All in due time, my dear." Then he leaned in and whispered something in her ear. Mary couldn't hear what was said, but she saw a new look of resolution in Charlotte's eyes. She waited as her friend stepped onto the ladder.

Before Mary could say goodbye, Pickney lowered his head. "It will be an honor to serve you as queen."

"Thank you, Pickney." She blushed. "For everything." She quickly hugged him before following Charlotte through the exit.

Shielding her eyes, she stepped into the bright sunshine. Everything seemed more vibrant after being in the dark for so long. The grass was still wet with morning dew. She quickly stood and brushed off her dress. Humberly and Charlotte were already hunched over on a log, examining the map.

"We'll be walking into enemy territory soon, so we must be very careful," he advised when they were all together. "Luckily, we're only a short distance from the location of the crown so we won't have far to go."

The expression on his face was serious as he re-folded the map. "The henchmen should be far behind us now, but I won't be satisfied until the Meir are summoned." He rose from the moss-covered log and walked briskly in the direction outlined. Mary and Charlotte could sense the urgency and hurried to keep up.

Despite the absence of a designated trail, the forest was fairly easy to navigate. With a long stick, Humberly moved vines and branches aside, making a path through the brush. The scenery was refreshing after being underground, and it reminded the girls of the Albright's backyard.

They walked in silence until a crisp breeze made Charlotte's arms break out in goosebumps. The sky above showed dark patches moving in. A fat raindrop landed on her head.

"I think we need our hoods." Looking back at Mary, she noticed the brooch glowing again. "Careful, the rain might make us melt," she said with a grin.

Mary looked down. "Not again." She sighed.

Humberly stopped alongside them taking out his rain gear. "Unfortunately, there isn't any shelter out here."

They hurried to put on their cloaks as the rain fell harder. He opened his umbrella, inviting the others to join him. "This is the size of a boat," Charlotte commented.

"It's as large as I need it to be."

"You mean it's enchanted, too? Cool."

They gathered their satchels, and he re-checked the compass to make sure they were still on course. Suddenly, a long howl sounded nearby. Humberly stiffened. "That sounded close," Mary remarked nervously.

"Indeed." Scanning the woods, he handed off the umbrella and took a small knife from his pocket. "Stay alert."

They walked on apprehensively, startled by the slightest sound. Mary clutched Charlotte's arm as she held onto the umbrella. "I guess the brooch was right this time," she whispered. The wind moaned eerily through the trees as lightning streaked the sky. Thunder sounded a few miles off. "Should we go back to the tunnels?" Mary asked, longing for safety.

Humberly considered her suggestion. "If they haven't caught our scent, we might be able to make it."

Before they could decide, however, a thick twig snapped behind them, making them freeze. A throaty growl cut through the storm. "I think we're too late," she said with a grimace.

Turning around, they found themselves face-to-face with a large gray wolf. Its dark hair stood on end while it snarled, bearing long, sharp teeth. Mary dug her fingers into Charlotte's arm, unaware she was holding her breath.

As another wolf appeared in the same menacing stance, Humberly searched for an escape. He found, however, that they were already surrounded. The pack closed in as Charlotte shouted frantically, "Use the stunning powder! Make us invisible! Do something!"

Yet he remained still. "The powder will only make them angrier, and they already know we're here. We have to fight."

The girls tried not to panic as they desperately searched for weapons. Grabbing a long branch covered with pine needles, Charlotte held it with one hand while using the umbrella to shield them with the other. Mary quickly picked up two large stones but still felt completely defenseless.

"Now, now," Humberly soothed as the leader of the pack drew closer. "We're just passing through." The rest of the animals remained in a circle, leaving no room to flee. He tightened his grip on the knife, knowing an attack was inevitable. He didn't have to wait long.

Almost immediately, the wolf lunged at his throat, knocking the umbrella from Charlotte's hands. Dodging its fangs just in time, Humberly slashed its shoulder causing it to yelp and tumble to the ground. Stumbling to its feet, it limped backward but continued to growl.

Humberly knew he wouldn't be able to hold them off for long. His only hope was that the girls could escape while he fought the pack. Watching the blade closely, the wolves paced back and forth waiting for an opportunity. Even though he could readily defend himself, he couldn't watch every direction at once.

The wolves soon took full advantage of this. While some continued to snap at Humberly, thoroughly distracting him, others set their sights on the easier targets, drawing closer to the girls.

Charlotte braced the branch in front of her, while Mary's fists held tightly to the rocks. At first, the wolves seemed to be toying with them, snapping at their clothing and grappling with the pine branch. They appeared to enjoy the shrieks of distress they caused.

However, after Charlotte managed to hit one across the head and cause it to stagger, the amusement stopped. The beasts' eyes narrowed and their snarls turned fierce. The largest one bit off the end of the branch in an instant, while another tore a piece from Mary's dress. They were making it clear that they were done playing.

When one finally sprang at Mary, panic gripped her. She threw her hands in front of her, letting the rocks fall to the ground. She was sure it was all over.

Hearing a loud squeal, she feared it had gotten Charlotte instead. She forced her eyes open and saw her friend still standing beside her while the wolf lay at her feet, a long arrow through its chest. Humberly and Charlotte seemed just as stunned.

Seeing their companion fall, the others began backing off. With a few still snarling, the leader threatened one last growl before limping away. Soon, they were alone once again, listening to the howls in the distance.

Mary stood frozen with shock. The dead animal in front of them was no longer a threat but she shivered at how close she'd come to being the one lying on the ground. Charlotte put her hand on Mary's shoulder, breathing heavily. "You okay?"

She nodded in disbelief. "Who shot the arrow?"

Humberly pushed the wolf over with his foot. Pulling the arrow from its chest, he studied the symbol engraved on the shaft. "The sign of a Bowmik. I didn't think there were any trained men left."

The girls waited for an explanation. "The Bowmik were, or are, a group of warriors that originated ages ago. They defended Ilyor and were said to never lose a battle, passing down their skills from one generation to the next. However, as the kingdom remained peaceful for so long, many lost interest in the art of warfare and followed other pursuits, allowing the tradition to end. If we had continued the custom, we probably wouldn't be where we are today."

"But, where is the Bowmik? I don't see anyone," Charlotte observed.

Humberly looked up into the trees. "If it truly was a Bowmik, he will only be seen if he wishes. And it appears that today, he does not."

After lingering for a time, he raised the arrow in salute and set it down to be re-claimed before striding away.

Mary and Charlotte were still too baffled to move. *Who was this mysterious person who had saved their lives? Had he been watching the whole time?* They hoped to catch a glimpse of the secret warrior through the trees. One thing they knew for sure, was they felt much safer knowing he was out there.

Finally, after shaking herself off and retrieving the umbrella, Mary took Charlotte's arm. "Let's go."

Charlotte nodded. Stealing one last glance, she shouted, "Thank you, whoever you are!"

Huddling under the umbrella again, they walked on beside Humberly. Their moods had grown somber since this last encounter, and they hoped the wolves wouldn't return to finish them off.

"The location of the crown will be in a large clearing," Humberly said, disrupting their thoughts.

"I was hoping it'd be in the castle," Charlotte said. Even though she was sure more dangers awaited them inside, at least there would be stone walls between them and those sharp fangs.

"Not much longer."

Looking for the next clearing offered a good distraction from their worries. When it began to downpour, and the thunder drew nearer, their focus shifted entirely to the threat of being struck by lightning. Every time the sky exploded, the girls would shudder and huddle closer together.

After walking a short distance, he stopped and looked at them. The storm was now so loud, that he had to yell to be heard. "According to the map, the crown should be hidden nearby."

But even he seemed unconvinced. Standing in a small nook, they were surrounded by trees. Nothing about this particular spot appeared any different than the others they'd gone through, except possibly being a bit wider.

"Are you sure this is the right place?" Mary half-yelled above the noise.

Holding the umbrella in one hand, he opened the map again. "As far as I can tell."

Reluctantly, the girls ducked out from their covering. They brushed old leaves and debris aside in hopes of discovering a mark of some kind. The pouring rain made it difficult to see anything. Tracing the tree trunks with their hands, they pushed on various bumps to no avail. Their disappointment continued to grow as the muddy clearing revealed no sign of a hiding place.

"Maybe this is the wrong area," Charlotte finally said. Both girls were now soaked and covered in mud. She pushed the matted hair from her forehead and walked over to Mary.

Mary, who had taken her glasses off because of the rain, could only see a blur coming toward her. Suddenly, the blur stumbled, crashing into her. She let out a cry as she fell backward. Reaching out with both arms, she felt the ground pass her by as it opened up and swallowed them both.

Hearing their shrieks, Humberly glanced up. "Oh good, you found it." He took his time folding the map and taking down his umbrella. Then he walked over and slid down to join them. A moment later, the ground closed above.

"Nice work, girls."

Charlotte groaned as she rolled over and eventually picked herself up off the ground.

"What happened?" Mary croaked, having had the wind knocked out of her.

"I tripped," Charlotte recalled, "and then the ground was gone." She leaned against the wall and felt a bug tickle her ear. She swatted at it but missed.

"Whatever you tripped over must have triggered the opening," Humberly noted.

"I guess we found the clue then. Is this one of the Drollmins' caves?"

"I believe they only dug to the point we exited last. This must be the work of another."

Charlotte swatted at the bug again. "So, how are we supposed to get out?"

"I'm sure there's a way."

Grazing her a third time, Charlotte snatched at the insect, finally getting hold of it. Unexpectedly, the ground opened above.

"Oh, thank goodness!" Mary said with a gasp. "I thought we were stuck down here."

Humberly looked up. "How did that happen?"

"I thought this was a bug," Charlotte said still holding the annoyance.

In the light, they could see it was a gnarled cord. She let it go and the light disappeared again. "Clever." Humberly removed a leather strap from his satchel and tied it to the cord, making it longer and hopefully easier to find. "We can exit the same way we came in. Now, let's see where this cave takes us."

Charlotte took the flashlight from her bag. The light proved the tunnel wasn't built nearly as well as the Drollmin's. It was at least big enough to move through though. They walked along for some time, keeping an eye out for anything out of place.

Suddenly, Charlotte stumbled on a protruding stone, causing the flashlight to fly from her hand and skid across the packed dirt floor. It flickered a few times and went out. Spots from the previous glow clouded their vision.

Charlotte pulled herself off of the ground. "Are you alright?" Mary asked.

Charlotte mumbled, "Yes, but now what?"

Since Humberly was the only one who could see in the dark, he led the way. The girls followed slowly, using the wall as their guide. The tunnel was crudely dug and once again, they were surrounded by dirt. They preferred it now, though, to being out in the storm with wild animals.

"It's kind of creepy down here," Mary admitted. "I wish there were torches on the walls like the other tunnels."

"That would be ideal," Humberly agreed.

She ran her hand along the wall and felt the dirt slide underneath her fingernails. Bits of soil from the ceiling dislodged at times, speckling her hair and clothing. She would definitely need a bath after this.

When something unexpectedly wiggled beneath her hand, she squealed and jumped back, bumping into Charlotte.

"What's wrong?"

"Something moved!"

"It's probably just a worm." Charlotte shrugged. "I found a few of them already."

The darkness hid Mary's look of disgust. She hated touching bugs of any kind, especially slimy ones. "I think I'll hold your arm instead."

After groping around for her shoulder, they moved forward, occasionally tripping over unlevel chunks of dirt. Eventually, Charlotte felt the texture of the wall change, abruptly becoming hard and smooth. Soon, their footsteps began to echo as well.

"It seems the tunnel has turned to stone," Humberly noted.

"Which means no more worms," Mary replied happily. A pale light streaked the path ahead.

"We're coming up on something."

They strained to see further, but the light was so soft that it was hard to tell if their eyes were deceiving them. Suddenly, a loud clatter reverberated down the chamber, stopping them in their tracks.

Not moving a muscle, they waited. The noise was a fresh reminder that they had no idea what they were walking into. Finally, after what seemed like an eternity, Humberly very cautiously moved forward. He only hoped the light didn't turn out to be the glow of the henchmens' torches waiting for them.

Chapter Fifteen

The Final Mark

As they drew closer, a large archway stood carved into the wall. The source of light was coming from within the center of the arch. Sidling up to the edge, Humberly peered around the corner. Multiple chests were scattered across the room but, fortunately, not one of the king's henchmen was in sight.

Relieved, they stepped into the space, finding well-lit lanterns hanging from the ceiling, and a layer of dust covering everything in sight. The floor and ceiling were carved from stone. The craftsmanship was nothing compared to the expert work of the Drollmin.

"Someone must have been here recently if the lanterns are still lit," Mary said worriedly.

"Not necessarily," Humberly said. "Notice there are no footprints in the dust. The lanterns are most likely filled with a substance called Eminesense. It provides a strong glow while rarely burning out."

Walking to the middle of the room, Charlotte noticed a broken vase on the floor. She turned it over and watched two mice scurry away. "I think we found where the noise came from."

Humberly dusted off the lid of the chest closest to him and examined the engraving. "This is the King's insignia. We must be in the royal treasury."

He tried the lock but it wouldn't budge. "I wouldn't normally deface another's property, but for the sake of the kingdom, I'll make an exception."

Taking what looked like a screwdriver from his bag, he secured it through the latch, prying it open. The hinges creaked as the lid lifted. An uneasy feeling settled in his stomach. Nothing. Not one jewel or coin to be found.

"What's wrong?" Mary joined him beside the chest. "Oh. Well, maybe there's something in the other chests."

Humberly nodded, but he wasn't optimistic. If someone went to the trouble to lock one empty chest, they were likely to do the same with the others. When he'd finished opening the last one, he let out a deflated sigh. "Empty. Every last one of them. The king must have had everything moved."

Mary closed the last lid slowly. "Does the map give any more clues?"

"The 'X' in the clearing was the last mark. We're on our own now."

Charlotte paced the floor, kicking up clouds of dust. "But why would he move the crown and not the gems? It doesn't make any sense."

"Maybe the crown was the only one he could find," Mary reasoned. "It would be nearly impossible to uncover the gems without their glowing."

Charlotte was thoughtful. "What good is the crown without the gems?"

"Perhaps we'll have better luck at the castle," Humberly suggested. "I believe we're only wasting our time here."

Charlotte had a feeling there was something they were missing. "I think that's what they want us to believe," she said. "There has to be another hiding place." Determined, she began to scour the area. If it took accidentally stumbling on a root to open the entrance to the cave, along with plenty of other hidden things to come this far, then maybe there was a secret trick here too.

The others watched as she studied the room. Along with the chests, and the one broken pot, the lights were the only objects. She climbed on a trunk to examine the bulbs. They all held what looked to be moving green, glowing slime. She didn't dare touch it.

Getting down on her knees, she swept the dust and dirt from the floor. Seeing how long this might take, the others began to help. Feeling even filthier than before, they finally stood up to inspect their work. A wave of discouragement swept over Charlotte. Not even one stone appeared out of place.

Hiding her frustration, she turned toward the walls. If there was a hidden notch, she was going to find it. She ran her hands over the surface, while the others did the same. They pushed and pulled on every crevice and bump there was, using the trunks to reach the highest spaces. By the time they made it to the third wall, their fingers were bruised and sore.

"Maybe we are just wasting time," she finally admitted.

"Possibly," Humberly said. "But we won't know until we finish."

Charlotte smiled, surprised by his change of heart. They each took a different section of the wall, and starting from the top, worked their way down.

It wasn't until they were near the bottom that Mary felt something unusual. Placing her hand on the stone again she gasped and pulled away. It was so strange she thought she was imagining it. But there was no denying the block was abnormally warm. It was a stark contrast to the cold stone around it. Taking a step back, there appeared to be a shallow imprint.

"I think I found something!"

Humberly excitedly brushed past Charlotte while Mary stepped out of the way. "How did you see this? It's hardly visible."

"The stone is warmer than the others."

He touched the stone with his paw. To him, it felt just as cool as the rest of the wall. Tracing the "X" symbol on the stone, he found the center slightly raised. He pushed his paw on it firmly and was delighted to hear a small click. After letting go, the entire slab moved a few inches forward.

Altogether, they worked the slab loose and set it down. "Would you like to do the honors?" Humberly asked Charlotte. Charlotte bent down and using quite a bit of her strength, pushed the heavy top off onto the floor. Unlike the chests, the interior of the slab was lined in rich velvet. A silk cloth lay over the contents.

Humberly nodded to Mary. With her stomach in her throat, she reached down and drew back the silky fabric. Underneath sat a stunning glass crown. "Oh, my!" she breathed.

"This crown hasn't been seen in ages," Humberly said happily. Then, unable to stop himself, he scooped Charlotte up and spun her around. "We never would have found it if you hadn't been so stubborn!"

"Uh, thanks I guess."

"I mean that in the most complimentary way, of course."

They all laughed as he turned back around. "The hidden compartment must have kept the king from finding this." He carefully lifted it from its resting place.

"I thought the gems we found went in the crown, but this already has gems," Mary noticed.

"I believe these are the false stones the evil son had installed in hopes of provoking its power."

"I'm glad it didn't work." Mary admired the way it mirrored the light, casting small rainbows around the room. She couldn't wait to see it in its full glory. "Can we put the real ones in now?"

Charlotte nodded eagerly in agreement.

"It may be best to wait," Humberly said thoughtfully. "If the king's men catch up to us, we wouldn't want them to have the crown and the real jewels at the same time."

The girls sighed in disappointment, and after waiting so long, he felt a little disappointed himself, but he knew it was the right decision. "I suppose it wouldn't hurt to at least envision it." Turning to Mary, he bowed. "Your majesty."

Mary couldn't hide her pleasure as he set the crown on her head. All at once, everything seemed different. She could feel a strength run through her that she had never known before. She was no longer afraid of what it meant to rule a kingdom. She knew she was born to do it.

Charlotte saw the change come over her and knew Mary wasn't the same timid girl who started this adventure. "You look radiant," she whispered. Mary smiled and squeezed her arm.

"I feel radiant." Even though she had been terrified to begin the journey, she now felt confident and secure. Wearing the crown gave her the strength to finally accept her calling.

After a minute or two, Humberly interrupted. "We should be going now. Keep it in your satchel, and I'll leave the gems in mine. If they catch up to us before we reach the castle, we'll have to split up."

Mary reluctantly removed the crown and tucked it securely in her bag. She was surprised that she could still feel its lasting effects. She turned to the others, ready to face whatever came next.

Humberly wasted no time. Covering the silk cloth in Eminesense as a makeshift torch, he handed it to Mary. "Finding the crown took longer than expected. We'll have to make our way to the castle quickly. By now, the henchmen have secured the false gem in the mine and will likely go straight to the castle."

Having the Eminesense as a light to guide them, they made it to the end of the tunnel much faster this time. The pull cord was easy to find, and they climbed to the surface.

"Which way?" Mary asked.

"It's not far from here. First, we'll drink the vanishing serum. It will take time to set in, but it will be imperative once we reach the darkest lands. Hopefully, it will last until we've completed our task."

Charlotte felt a pang of guilt knowing she'd been the one to open the aged liquid at the beginning of their adventure. Thankfully, Humberly didn't harp on this fact. He quickly removed his satchel and retrieved the new vial.

"Okay. Only take a mouthful. We mustn't waste a drop." After they each took a swig, he added a drop of serum to their satchels. They continued moving for a while. They were near the edge of the dark lands when Humberly finally stopped.

"We'll eat here while we wait for the serum to take full effect."

Mary and Charlotte were happy to rest their legs after traveling all morning. Sitting on a fallen log, they ate slowly, giving the mixture more time to set in. The warmth of the sun began drying their damp clothes. While taking the last bite of her apple, Charlotte noticed her fingers were gone. "I think it's starting to kick in." Humberly's leg had disappeared and Mary was missing her left arm.

"I don't think I'll ever get used to this," Mary admitted.

Taking out a thin rope already dosed with serum, Humberly tied it to each of them. "To keep anyone from getting lost once we're invisible," he explained. After packing their things, it wasn't long before they each disappeared. "From now on, we must be as quiet as possible."

Charlotte and Mary whispered their agreement. They felt a gentle tug on the line as he walked forward. He moved slowly at first, careful not to pull the rope too hard. But soon they were walking in a steady rhythm.

It was very obvious when they stepped into the darkest lands. The forest itself became dim and gloomy. Shadows grew longer, causing rotten trees and overgrown shrubs to take on eerie forms. Black vultures circled overhead waiting for something to die.

Shudders ran up and down the girls' spines. With wide eyes, they scanned the forest at every snapping twig or rustling leaf, making a point to stay as close to Humberly as possible. They could only hope the wolves didn't pick up their scent again.

When the tension was nearly unbearable, the top of the large, stone castle finally emerged. They were less than a mile away when they trudged down a steep embankment and into an open field. As they drew closer, it was easy to see the castle had long been neglected.

Wild vines and moss obscured most of the white stone, while other areas were beginning to crumble. The untamed land had claimed the building as its own. "This was once the most beautiful structure in the kingdom," Humberly noted sadly. "Now, it's near ruins."

The trio stood for a moment gazing at the forsaken fortress. Mary never thought a castle could look so dreary. She hoped she wouldn't have to live there. Feeling an abrupt pull on the line, she knew it was time to move on.

Humberly's knowledge of the grounds proved invaluable as he steered them through a labyrinth of unkempt hedges, far from any castle guards at their posts. After crossing a large vegetable garden, they finally came to the servants' entrance.

The trio stood to the side of the locked door and waited. The plan was to slip in when someone exited. It was some time before a servant carrying a bushel of tomatoes came up the path. As she opened the door, one of the tomatoes fell to the ground.

Instinctively, Mary bent down to pick it up. Charlotte felt the pull of the rope and guessed what she was doing. She reached out and caught Mary's arm just in time. Realizing her mistake, Mary let out a small gasp.

The woman grabbed the tomato and looked up suspiciously. She scanned the area wondering where the noise had come from. The uninvited guests stood as still as possible. After several moments passed, she finally went on her way inside.

Seeing his opportunity, Humberly lunged through the doorway, practically dragging the girls behind him. Charlotte, who was the last in line, had to push the door back to make it through in time. Once inside, they all huddled next to a stone pillar.

"What happened?" Humberly demanded.

"I wasn't thinking," Mary said. She heard him sigh and was grateful she couldn't see what was sure to be a stern look on his face.

"Never mind. Only try to be more careful moving forward." This was his only reproach before changing the subject. "We must get to the throne room for Mary to summon the Meir," he whispered. "I was rarely allowed there during my time here, so I'm not as familiar with the direction. But I believe we need to ascend the stairs and head down the corridor."

The girls followed him up the stairs, staying as close to the inner wall as possible. The second floor led down a long corridor with only a few guards scattered throughout. Charlotte was glad the serum was still working.

They tip-toed past the guards while holding their breath. Garbled talk and laughter poured through a partially cracked doorway. Carefully, Humberly peeked in only to find the large dining area. "I must not remember as clearly as I thought," he said apologetically. "We'll have to turn back."

Several other corridors provided no better luck. As they turned down yet another hall, Charlotte felt an itch on her leg. She reached down to scratch it and noticed her bootlace was untied. "Hold on a sec," she told the others.

Turning toward her, Mary reached out for Humberly. "Charlotte's legs! I can see them!" Charlotte froze when she realized what was happening. The others were both still completely invisible.

Humberly rushed to take out more serum, while Mary frantically kept watch. A moment later, they heard heavy footsteps coming down the hall. Charlotte's head and legs were almost fully visible by this point.

Desperately searching for a place to hide, she tucked herself into a nearby door frame and pulled out Annabel's perfume. She figured there was no better time to test it than now.

As the footsteps drew closer, she squeezed her eyes shut, hoping to blend in. Unfortunately, it didn't work. "What do you think you're doing here?" The guard shouted, noticeably confused by her appearance.

Charlotte jumped and sprayed the perfume in his face. He sputtered for a few seconds and wiped his eyes. For a moment he stood still, and she thought the perfume might be working. Then he roared, "You're coming with me!"

Her face fell in disappointment. She tried to protest but he refused to listen. Unsure where to seize, he put his hand tightly around her neck and dragged her down the hall.

Chapter Sixteen

Book of Verses

Charlotte allowed herself to be led away as she fumbled to untie the rope. She didn't want the others to get caught along with her. It was disheartening that the perfume hadn't worked, but she figured it was all the more reason not to trust Annabel.

The guard pulled her down the steps, barely letting her find her footing, while he roughly explained the punishment for intruders. Her stomach turned at the thought of spending even a few days in the dungeon. The stairwells spiraled down further and further, making it seem like the circles would never end. "Shouldn't the king decide whether I'm thrown into the dungeon or not?" she pleaded.

He laughed as though she'd made a joke. "The king has no time for meddling children." His grip around her neck tightened, making her wince. She hoped Humberly would be able to find her once they freed the kingdom.

Finally, the spinning stopped. The air turned cold and clammy, making her shiver. He was taking a large key from his pocket when a strange look came over his face. He put his hand to his ear and shook his head in confusion. Suddenly, his grip around Charlotte's neck loosened, and he turned to face her.

"Where is it you'd like to go, Miss?"

Charlotte was stunned by his sudden change in manner and began to stutter. "Uh, t-to the throne room?" It came out as more of a question than a command.

"Right away."

She followed in bewilderment before realizing the perfume must be working. *Maybe Annabel is trustworthy after all,* she thought. *Although it certainly didn't work "immediately" like she had claimed.* She felt a squeeze on her arm.

"How did you do that?" Mary asked.

Charlotte didn't answer for fear of being overheard, but she was relieved to know she wasn't alone. They climbed back up the many flights of stairs and turned down several corridors as he led them to the throne room. After pushing open the large doors, he ushered her through.

"Where's the king?" she asked.

"He's in the dining hall. Would you like me to summon him?"

"No!" she responded too quickly. "I mean, that won't be necessary."

"Is there anything else I can do for you, Miss?"

"Um, no, thank you. That will be all." She tried to sound as grown up as possible. He left the room, closing the door behind him.

"Well, you certainly have a gift for persuasion," Humberly remarked. His paws were now visible, but he had cleverly hidden them behind her while the guard was around. Mary had found it hard not to laugh at the two paws floating in mid-air.

"Now comes your part, Mary. Charlotte can help you replace the gems before you call the Meir. I must go prepare the Book of Verses."

He left them to fit the gems and began studying the large book on the podium. The girls worked hurriedly to replace the stones, with the help of Humberly's screwdriver. Each time they did, the crown would act like a magnet, pulling the genuine gem into place.

They had just placed the last jewel when the doors flew open abruptly. Mary was startled, and the crown fell from her hands. She quickly reached to grab it but was too late. Rolling unsteadily across the floor, it stopped at King Obsidious' feet. The glow of the gems had already begun to dim as it moved farther away from Mary. Pleasure filled the king's cold blue eyes as he calmly bent down to retrieve the prize.

"I see you've found my crown," he remarked, walking to the center of the room. "And with all of its adornments too." He examined the now fully visible girls. His large stature was intimidating enough without his gaze directed at them. "You wouldn't be the ones trying to displace me, would you?" He smirked. "I wonder how you made it this far."

Mary glanced at Charlotte, but neither of them knew what to say. "Don't worry. Whoever helped you will be dealt with soon enough." Spinning on his heel, he walked to the throne and turned to face the room. Humberly had quickly hidden behind a pillar and was hurriedly searching for the right inscription in the book.

"Now, this is a crown fit for a king!" He spoke to no one in particular. "Hidden away for all these years. But now, thanks to you, I will finally take my rightful place over the entire kingdom." Mary held her breath.

"Sire," the guard who entered with him spoke haltingly, "with the highest respect, only the rightful heir can wear the crown without being harmed."

The king's face turned grim. "And am I *not* the rightful heir?" he bellowed.

"Of course, Sire, I didn't mean..." he trailed off under his withering gaze.

"There are those," he gave the guard a sideways glance, "who still refuse to recognize my supremacy. However, as the most powerful king to ever rule Ilyor, I have more than proven my worth. At the very least, the crown will certainly sense I am worthier than some insignificant child."

King Obsidious raised the crown with a look of insatiable greed. He placed it firmly on his head, hesitating only a moment before turning to the girls in triumph. "What did I tell you? No one is more worthy than I!" He began to laugh wildly.

Fear gripped the pair as they realized they had failed. Charlotte stepped back with trembling knees while Mary clung to her for support. Humberly peeked out from behind the pillar with an expression of grievance. It was impossible the crown could approve of such a devious man, and yet still nothing happened.

Mary grimaced as King Obsidious moved forward. *Would the Meir follow his lead? Was Humberly mistaken about me being meant to rule?* Her thoughts ran wild as he demanded the two captives be taken to the dungeon.

"Lock them in the innermost cell to be sure they never escape." He looked at the guard coldly. "I'll deal with you later."

"Yes, Sire." He avoided the king's eyes as he took hold of the prisoners.

"My time has finally come." Obsidious walked to the podium and opened the book Humberly had wisely returned. His hand fell heavily on the open page before him. "Now, nothing will be able to stop me." Lifting it off of the podium, he began to recite the verses. His voice was gruff. Halfway through, the gems began to glow.

"It's working!" Charlotte whispered. Mary squeezed her hand. Even the guard stopped at the door to watch in amazement. The gems increased in vibrancy. Outside of the castle, dark clouds tumbled across the sky, and a strong gust of wind threw open the castle windows. Debris swept in, cluttering the throne room. It felt as if a hurricane was forming around them.

King Obsidious was shouting above the noise. More guards hurried into the room, wondering at the commotion. When he finished reading, he yelled into the storm, "Today, Meir, you will follow your king!" He raised both hands in the air, waiting for his power to be unleashed.

The wind whipped around him, howling loudly as if responding to his call. The girls braced themselves and awaited the inevitable when suddenly, Obsidious' face froze. He slumped onto the podium with an agonizing groan. The other guards ran to help him.

"What's happening?" Mary glanced around. Everyone looked as confused as she felt. With the guards trying to carry him away, the king abruptly collapsed. He let out a loud yell, before disintegrating into a pile of ash. And all at once, he was gone.

The crown clattered to the floor, while his sentries stared in disbelief at what had taken place. Their dazed looks eventually changed to ones of clarity. After the wind swept up the king's remains, the weather returned to normal. The guard's grip around the girls loosened, and he stepped back.

The head guard came forward and picked up the crown, unsure what to make of the young rescuers. "We've been under a spell these many years," he started, "forced to submit to the king's orders." He looked up at Mary and Charlotte. "Thank you for setting us free."

"You're welcome," Charlotte said boldly, while Mary smiled sheepishly.

"I believe it's time," Humberly said, stepping out from behind the pillar, "for the rightful heir to take her place."

The same man turned toward him. "After all this time? Who is the rightful heir?"

Humberly didn't answer, he just turned toward Mary. "You're up, my dear." She stared at him in disbelief.

"Didn't you just see what happened?"

"Yes, but the same won't happen to you." Mary was unconvinced. "The king was unable to separate his vanity from the truth. He was never meant to rule. But you are not like the king. Now, go take your place." Mary borrowed an ounce of Humberly's confidence and stepped forward. The two went together to the podium.

She drew in a shaky breath and took the crown held out to her. As soon as she did, the gems began glowing intensely. Loud gasps sounded across the room. As she stepped up, she felt her courage growing. Humberly stood beside her and pointed to the weathered page she was to read.

Closing her eyes tightly, she placed the crown on her head and let out a deep breath before scanning the faded inscription. At first, it was difficult to make out the words. But as she began to read, they came alive, expanding right before her. Her speech grew stronger with each verse, as it seemed as though it were written just for her.

Halfway through her reading, the doors were hurled open. Immediately, she ducked down with the book in her hands. She was glad she did when she saw a man in a familiar dark cloak hobble forward. Walking angrily to the center of the room, he threw back his hood.

"Stop!" he shouted brazenly. "What is this evil you have done, murdering the king?" He turned toward the guards. "Arrest these impostors at once!" They stood back, aware of Delirion's power, but making no move to obey his command.

"We didn't murder the king!" Charlotte cried out. Delirion spun around with an icy glare, causing her to shrink back. When he spotted the perfume bottle still in her hand, a twisted smile formed on his face.

"Such a naïve little one," he said, chuckling to himself. "Tell me," he paused, "did you enjoy Annabel's little gifts?"

Charlotte's mouth dropped open as she looked down in confusion. "You? But the perfume worked. Why would you help us?"

"Oh?" He smirked. "Senseless girl. The guard obeyed *my* command, not yours. Have you not yet realized, everyone is under my control?"

Charlotte took a step back, glancing at Mary. "The brooch. It wouldn't have warned us when danger was coming then," she whispered. "But what was the point?" Realization suddenly dawned on her and she gasped. "It led the danger *to* us, didn't it?"

Delirion laughed. "Now you see."

"Keep reading," Humberly whispered. He stepped down from the platform as Delirion grew bored of taunting Charlotte and turned away. "You've darkened this kingdom long enough, Delirion," he said, getting his attention. "Today, Ilyor will be restored."

The robed figure sneered. He began circling Humberly, his staff striking the floor with every step. "You seem to believe you've already won. Foolish beast. Obsidious was nothing more than a puppet in my hands." He stretched out his bony hand in a tight fist as though it were crushing something.

He continued speaking in a low, confident voice. "The darkness cannot be overcome so easily. It's grown too strong for even the Meir to fight." He shifted his body in preparation. "You will all be prisoners for the rest of your miserable lives—or die!"

He raised his staff to strike, but Humberly leaped out of the way putting more space between them. The staff landed firmly on the ground, making Delirion seethe. With a sudden twist of his wrist, a streak of lightning shot from the rod toward his opponent. Humberly stumbled, grabbing his arm where the bolt had grazed him.

All at once, Delirion noticed Mary, hiding behind the podium with the open book. The glowing gems filled his eyes with terror. Suddenly, another jolt charged toward the book, ripping it in two. Grabbing a shield from a nearby statue, Humberly leaped forward, sharply bringing its edge down on the staff. A loud crack echoed throughout the room.

Delirion dropped to his knees. He clenched the broken pieces, enraged. Then, fixing his eyes on Humberly, he removed a small dagger from its sheath and stood to his feet. "Ilyor's loyalty will remain to *me*," he said through clenched teeth.

Meanwhile, Mary frantically beat the book with her cloak, putting out the fire. Thankfully the bolt came at an angle and barely missed her cheek before hitting its target. She could still feel the warmth from its passing.

The pages lay in singed fragments, with the cover destroyed. Finding pieces of what appeared to be the marked page, Mary saw that more than half the sheet was missing. Charlotte rushed over and stooped down to help. Together, they sorted through the scattered pages for the missing half. Noticing a flap out of the corner of her eye, Mary glanced over and snatched a piece stuck between the wall and the pillar. She smiled with relief and quickly began reading.

While Mary read, Charlotte watched helplessly as the two rivals sparred. The few guards left in the room viewed the fight with a mixture of uncertainty and fear, waiting to see if Humberly could prevail.

Delirion moved forward, taking jabs liberally, while Humberly nimbly defended himself. This continued until Humberly tripped on the broken staff, momentarily losing his balance. Seizing the opportunity, Delirion lunged forward, knocking the shield from his hands and slashing Humberly's upper leg. He fell backward, struggling to get up.

As Delirion raised his knife for the final attack, a strong gust of wind, accompanied by a blinding light, filled the room. He cowered, shielding his eyes. "No!" His body writhed and fought as the wind lifted him and the knife fell from his hand. "No!" In a moment, without warning, he vanished. Everyone stared in amazement at the now empty space.

Finally, Humberly slunk back on the floor and Charlotte rushed to his side. When she ripped off a piece of her cloak to bind his leg, he groaned.

"Am I hurting you?" she asked.

"I'll be fine. But you just ruined a perfectly good cloak." Charlotte grinned and helped him to his feet. When Mary joined them, there were sparks of light dancing around her.

"I think they're happy," she said. The Meir were extremely grateful for their freedom, and the immense power they'd gained from the crown's restoration. She giggled with joy and Charlotte watched in wonder as Mary connected with the fascinating creatures.

Once they had thanked their queen, they rushed over to Humberly, healing each wound. Then, circling toward the ceiling they twirled and fluttered before exiting through the throne room doors.

Recognizing she hadn't taken a full breath up until now, Charlotte inhaled deeply. She eyed the others, who seemed just as stunned at the recent events as she was.

Turning toward Mary, Humberly bowed low. "Thank you, my queen." Trembling, the guards all quickly did the same. They were astonished by this child who claimed authority over the most powerful beings in the land.

Feeling a bit strange, Mary leaned into Charlotte, who started to bend a knee. She quickly grabbed her arm. "Don't you dare," she whispered. They both smiled and Charlotte wrapped her in a hug instead.

"You saved Ilyor!"

"*We* saved Ilyor," Mary corrected, knowing how much she relied on her friend's courage. "I couldn't have done any of this without you. Thanks for always believing in me."

Charlotte smiled at her friend. "I just helped you realize who you already were."

Humberly walked over, looking as confident as ever. "I'm relieved that's over, but it's no surprise how it ended. After all, it was your destiny to save

Ilyor." He looked at them together and smiled. "I'm very proud of you both. You served your kingdom well."

Chapter Seventeen

Crowning Ceremony

The next few days were a blur. After remembering his way around, Humberly quickly began the process of restoring the castle to order. The grateful servants followed his instructions, doting on Mary and Charlotte whenever they could. They were overjoyed at no longer being forced to serve Obsidious. Mary also made it clear they were welcome to leave if they wished, which of course only made them more eager to stay. The Meir were busy bringing what was dead back to life and undoing the destruction Delirion had caused, which overjoyed the kingdom.

A week after their victory, Mary awoke to a blaring sound. She sat up with a jolt. "Did the king come back?"

"No, no," Gertrude, the girls' personal dresser, reassured her. "It's only the kingdom rejoicing. We're forever grateful." She smiled before continuing to arrange their clothing.

"Oh, thank goodness." She fell back on the pillow with relief, accidentally waking Charlotte with a snort.

"Good morning," she said through a yawn.

"Good morning, Lady Charlotte." Gertrude dropped the item she was folding and excitedly turned to the armoire. "Now that you're both awake, I'll show you your dresses for this evening. I hope you don't mind, but I took the liberty of making them myself." She opened the armoire and took out a long, blue silk gown. Mary's mouth fell.

"I'm glad you approve," Gertrude said, smiling broadly before replacing it with the next gown. "And here is yours, Lady Charlotte." Charlotte reached over to touch the beautiful pink gown. She was glad hers didn't have a train to trip over like the other. Even in her short time knowing them, Gertrude already understood their unique styles.

After they each bathed, she helped them into their dresses. "I'm starting to see why Humberly was so appalled by my cat shirt," Charlotte commented, making Mary laugh.

"Maybe we should glue some fake gemstones onto these to really make them shine." Seeing a crease form on Gertrude's forehead, Mary quickly added, "We're only teasing, of course."

A short time later, Humberly came to escort them to the throne room. "Ahh, you both look stunning." He offered an arm to each of them, and they walked the halls, past the portraits of Ilyor's previous royalty. According to Humberly, the king had left them as evidence of his victory.

Before turning the corner, a certain picture captured Mary's attention. She wasn't sure why she felt drawn to it, but the green eyes and kind smile were strangely comforting.

"That looks like your dad," Charlotte commented.

Mary gasped. "You're right. I wondered why he looked familiar." She laughed.

"Well, these are your ancestors, right?"

"I hadn't really thought of that." She'd been so preoccupied with what it meant to be queen, that she'd forgotten she was related to this long line of royalty.

"I guess you know where your freckles come from now." Mary touched her face as realization dawned on her. She smiled, knowing this kingdom was as much a part of her as her own world.

Before reaching the open doors, Humberly paused. "Are you ready?" Mary took a deep breath and then nodded. Humberly had worked hard to prepare her for this moment. With the others behind her, she stepped through the doorway.

Instantly, everyone grew quiet. She cast a secret glance over the room and was thankful only the royal officials were present. Then, just as Humberly had instructed her, she moved toward the throne and gracefully turned to face her audience. The royal ambassador stood beside her. When he spoke, his rich voice filled the room.

"We have long awaited this moment. A rightful heir takes his or her place over the kingdom of Ilyor. And finally, through the noble bloodline, a successor has risen. Our new queen has proven herself worthy in every way, destroying the reign of darkness and establishing peace throughout the land. Because of this, we have each taken a solemn vow to serve our queen, through life or death, be it for the good of Ilyor."

He turned toward Mary. "Will you, Mary Elizabeth Albright, heir through the bloodline of Davenpore, accept your responsibilities as Queen of Ilyor, both in times of peace and times of war, always striving toward the prosperity of the kingdom?"

"I will." Then, handing her the royal scepter, he set the crown in place.

"I hereby present the Queen of Ilyor."

Applause echoed throughout the chamber as the glowing gems reflected into the crowd. Keeping her head still, her eyes searched the sea of people. When they landed on Charlotte, relief washed over her. She knew she would need Charlotte now more than ever.

Stepping down, Mary walked back through the open doorway while Humberly and Charlotte followed close behind. Later, the speech Humberly and she had prepared would be required during the gathering of the people, but for now, she could simply rest.

That evening, the banquet hall was filled with all who had journeyed to honor their new queen. Long tables, heaped with food, were lined down the middle of the room. Every seat was taken.

Charlotte peeked in and saw the Drollmin in the far corner, already preparing for a toast. She recognized many of the villagers they'd met in town too. A thrill of delight ran through her. She couldn't wait to start the celebration.

Humberly was giving final instructions to Mary, who was listening attentively. Charlotte moved to stand beside her. When he finished speaking, Mary nodded solemnly. "Open the doors."

On her command, the guards pulled back the heavy oak doors, bowing their heads as she passed. She looked regal walking into the banquet hall, her long train trailing behind her. Upon entering, she waited while her presence was announced. All at once, the chattering stopped. All eyes were fixated as she walked to the middle of the room. Being the center of attention made her stomach tighten. It took a few moments to gather her courage before speaking.

"When Charlotte and I first came to Ilyor, I knew nothing of its existence or my family's history. I was unaware of the long line of kings and queens which had gone before me, or of the trouble that darkened this incredible land. Even after meeting Humberly and learning of my place here, it felt as if it were only a dream. And to be honest, on the hardest parts of the journey, I wished it were." She paused to take in the room.

"However, the more I learned of Ilyor and those standing against the darkness, the more I admired this world and its people. Even after facing unbelievable hardships, they never lost hope. After meeting many of them, I knew I couldn't leave without doing everything possible to restore peace to this land. Ultimately, it was through the citizens of Ilyor, and my dear friends, that I came to finally accept my destiny.

"Therefore, as your queen, I promise to lead this kingdom as my ancestors did before me, with strength and dignity. I will accept the wise counsel of those devoted to Ilyor's future and will honor the customs of its people. Together, we will continue to conquer our enemies and we *will* be victorious. It is a privilege to be among you now celebrating the renewal of our kingdom. I am deeply honored to be your queen. To Ilyor!"

Cheers rang out, flooding the dining hall. "To Ilyor!"

"And to our queen!" Pickney shouted. Loud cheers broke out again as they toasted their new ruler. Mary breathed a sigh of relief as she sat at the head of her table. Humberly and Charlotte were already placed on either side.

"Well done," Humberly whispered, patting her hand.

She returned the smile. "I'm glad it's over."

"It's only one of many," he said and chuckled. "But you'll get used to it in time."

She scrunched up her nose while Charlotte filled her glass. "Just think, class presentations will be a cinch." Grinning, Mary realized how simple her life had been before coming to Ilyor. For a second, she wondered if it would ever be that simple again.

The conversation shifted when a server came to fill her plate. After taking the first bite, the rest of the crowd began to eat. Soon the room was filled with lively chatter and scraping utensils. Before long, Maribel came and scooped Mary and Charlotte into a bear hug. "I just knew you could do it! Come stay at my inn any time. Free of charge!" Then, just as quickly, she hurried off to help the servers, even though she was a guest.

Throughout the night, many others stopped to pay their respects as well. Some, who had been freed from the castle dungeons, could only kiss the girls' hands and weep in gratitude. In this, Mary and Charlotte could feel the weight of their actions. They shuddered to think what would've become of Ilyor if they'd abandoned their quest.

After dinner, the Drollmin dropped a large, heavy satchel on the table with a thump. "To begin your treasury," Pickney explained. They got up to hug them and were quickly swept away to a lively tune. It was the first dance of the night, and everyone clapped along while the girls kept up with the playful footwork.

By the next song, there was hardly enough space on the floor. Mary and Charlotte were passed from one partner to the next, thoroughly enjoying themselves.

It was long into the night when the Meir arrived, bringing with them beautiful music and fireworks. The guests were delighted by the unexpected visitors, and the celebration lasted throughout the evening and well into the morning.

By the time the last guest left, the sun was beginning to rise. Charlotte was already passed out on a couch, while Mary sat beside her, trying to keep her eyes open. She was determined to stay awake until everyone had gone. "Why don't you get some rest now, Your Majesty?" Humberly asked politely.

"That's fine, Humberly," she said, pulling herself up, "but please, just call me Mary."

"As you wish, Mary."

Chapter Eighteen

Home Again

When the girls awoke, it was early afternoon. The sun was streaming through the windows and the birds were chirping happily. Gertrude waited until they'd finished eating before helping them dress. Afterward, she led them to the main study where Humberly was sitting comfortably in an armchair. "Ahh, how did you girls sleep? I suppose I should refer to you as ladies now."

"Like I was on a bed of cotton." Charlotte flopped into the chair next to him. He smiled.

"We may need a few lessons on etiquette now that we're in the castle."

She sat up politely. "And maybe a few lessons on how to rule a kingdom."

"Yes, perhaps a few of those too. You both have much to learn."

"When do we start?" Mary asked eagerly.

"I'm afraid lessons will have to wait until your return to Ilyor. It's getting close to sunset in your world."

Her face fell. "I hate to leave just after becoming queen. I don't want the people to think I'm abandoning them."

"Don't worry, dear. The people know you belong to two worlds and have responsibilities to both. However, we do need to establish a representative while you're away. Now, I've made a list of the most noble men and women in the kingdom." He unrolled his scroll.

"Humberly," she interrupted, "I don't need to see a list."

He looked slightly perturbed. "I believe it's in Ilyor's best interest to appoint someone to oversee things in your absence."

"As queen, I know exactly what's in Ilyor's best interest." She took the scroll and began to roll it up.

"Of course, but you haven't even seen…"

"Which is why, I am appointing you, Sir Humberly, to run the kingdom in my absence."

His eyes grew wide. "But I'm not even a nobleman."

"I can think of no one more noble."

"I, I don't know what to say."

"That's a first," Charlotte said grinning.

"Say you'll accept."

He bowed low. "It would be my honor."

The rest of the afternoon was spent making the necessary arrangements for their absence.

The following morning, he woke the girls earlier than usual. "It's time. You can say your farewells during breakfast." Then he left them to get ready. Getting out of bed, they stood quietly as Gertrude helped them dress. Each was preoccupied with their thoughts about returning home. They couldn't help but have mixed feelings.

As they neared the dining room, Charlotte finally broke the silence. "Do you think normal life will ever be as good as being in Ilyor?"

"It will be different," Mary said, "but that doesn't mean it's bad. When we go home, we'll get to see our families, and we'll be able to just be kids again. Even if we're not as brave as we are now." She frowned.

Charlotte knew Mary was referring to herself and linked an arm through hers. "At least in our world, you won't have to face evil henchmen or overrule an awful king. You've always been as brave as you've needed to be."

She smiled, grateful for the encouragement, and realized Charlotte was right. Living in her own world was a lot easier than being a queen. And she always had the courage to do what was right before coming to Ilyor, which is what really mattered. They each entered the dining hall, feeling a little lighter than they had before.

Humberly greeted them as they came through the door. "Are you ready for your next adventure?"

Charlotte smirked. "I don't know if you can call going home an adventure, but I think we're ready."

"Good. You never know what tomorrow will bring."

"Will we have to walk back to the tree house?" Mary asked.

He shook his head. "There are portals all over Ilyor. Now that we're not following the map, we'll arrive at the Sycamore very quickly."

After eating breakfast and saying many goodbyes, they followed Humberly into the courtyard. "How much time will have passed in Ilyor if we stay a week in our world?" Mary asked worriedly.

"There's no need to worry about time."

"But we could miss a whole year here by then," Charlotte argued.

"Not with this." He took a beautiful silver bracelet from his pocket and clasped it onto Mary's wrist. "Since you're now officially queen, the time of Ilyor and that of your world will align, as long as you're wearing this. You can remove the bracelet any time you return to Ilyor so the time lasts longer here."

She touched the chain with its tiny crown charm. "That's wonderful," she breathed. "I promise to keep it safe."

"I know you will." He then handed them each a small brooch. Seeing the wary look on Mary's face, he reassured her, "Don't worry, these were made by the Drollmin. We'll use them to correspond while you're away. When I need to speak with you, your brooch will glow. Push it in firmly and hold it down to communicate."

Having nothing more to give them, he stepped behind a large statue of a lion. "When you're ready," he said with a gesture of his hand. Charlotte took one last glance at the castle, then moved to where he was pointing. She saw a flash of light and was suddenly standing in a large field of flowers. Once she felt steady, she looked around.

Recognition quickly dawned on her, and she stooped down to touch the soft white petals. Soon Mary and Humberly appeared beside her. They walked to the enchanted tree, which now seemed like a distant memory. Humberly touched a notch at the bottom, and the tree instantly began to grow.

"I'll wait here while you get your things." Making their way to the top, Mary unlocked the trap door with the key that had once again appeared in Humberly's pocket.

"It may not be a castle, but I think this is my favorite place in Ilyor," she said.

Charlotte nodded and they took their time changing into their own clothes.

"I'm going to miss this velvet dress," Mary said, hugging it to herself.

"And I'll miss these great boots." Charlotte held her foot up in the air, then let it fall to the floor with a thud. "It'll be strange being home again," she admitted sadly. "There wasn't enough time to get used to living in the palace."

Mary laughed. "That's the part I'm looking forward to the most. I won't have to make decisions for an entire kingdom."

"I don't know. With these brooches, you'll probably have to make some queenly decisions."

Mary rubbed the purple brooch pinned to her shirt. "That's true. But at least I won't be in the spotlight."

The girls finished getting ready and looked about the cottage. It was hard to believe the adventure was coming to an end. They'd learned so much in their time there, it felt as though they'd been gone a year.

"Come on," Mary said. "Humberly's waiting for us." Charlotte sighed and reluctantly followed her through the door.

"Do you have all of your things?" Humberly asked after they reached the bottom.

"I think so," Mary replied.

"And the communication devices?"

She pointed to the two brooches. Satisfied, he turned and led them through the wildflowers. With the sun warming their backs, they walked along leisurely, letting the flowers brush against their legs. Coming to the woods, Charlotte was surprised by the excitement she felt to go home. She was even eager to eventually meet her little sister. Suddenly, it occurred to her that Mary was right. Being home would be different and the changes might be scary at first, but she had things to appreciate in both worlds.

The journey had helped her realize a new baby didn't make her any less special, and there was plenty of room for both of them in their family. She smiled to herself knowing how fortunate she was.

It was easy to navigate the woods as Humberly guided them down a simpler path. When they passed the place where they'd had their picnic, the sandwich crust left on the stump was covered with ants. It was a strange feeling knowing they'd only been gone less than a day.

Humberly stopped right at the threshold. "This is where I leave you, ladies. It has been an honor journeying with you." He bowed his head, but they both moved in and hugged him tightly.

"I guess we'll see you again soon." Charlotte smiled.

"We'll miss you, Humberly," Mary added.

"And I'll miss you," came the reply. Finally, they turned to leave.

"Are you ready?" Mary asked, taking Charlotte's hand. She nodded. With a deep breath, they stepped over the threshold. The same queasy sensation swept over them. Charlotte held her stomach and groaned.

"At least it doesn't last long," Mary said when their stomachs had settled. When they turned to wave, they saw nothing but trees.

"He's already gone," Charlotte noted sadly. Mary put her arm around her.

"We'll see him again soon." Humberly watched as they picked up their bikes and started to leave. He was still standing right where they'd left him, merely invisible past the threshold. He smiled fondly at the girls who had risked so much to save his kingdom. He was already looking forward to their return.

"Race you home!" Charlotte challenged. They rode off laughing as Humberly finally turned to go.

After all of the exercise they'd had in Ilyor, the ride home was easy. They weren't even winded when they reached their street. "See you tomorrow, your Royal Highness," Charlotte called, riding up her driveway.

"It's just Mary to you!"

She dropped her bike on the lawn and ran through the front door. Her mom was talking in the kitchen and her brothers were already seated at the table.

"There you are!" Mrs. Jenkins said. Charlotte wrapped her arms around her mom's belly.

"What's this for?"

"I'm just excited to meet my baby sister," she answered, smiling up at her. Her mom squeezed her back. "I'm going to be the best big sister."

"Yes, you will, sweetheart. And we'll need your help now more than ever," she said, caressing her hair.

"Oh and can I get a pet fox?"

Mrs. Jenkins' eyebrows rose in surprise. "Why don't we talk about that later? Now, go wash up. You look like you've been playing in the woods all day."

You have no idea, she thought. When she took her place at the table, she looked around contentedly and realized just how homesick she'd been. She grinned when her brother threw a pea at her dad. *Humberly would not approve.* Thankfully, she didn't have to worry about etiquette here.

And even though she was thrilled to have finally had a real adventure, she was realizing ordinary life wasn't so ordinary after all. And in this moment, she couldn't imagine being anywhere else.

Acknowledgment

Thank you to my husband and son, Ricky and Levi, for your patience as this book took a great deal of time, for jumping in to help, and for years of support and encouragement.

My family and friends, who reviewed, suggested, proofread, allowed their kids to beta-read, and encouraged- I love you all.

Benjamin Wood, Emma Wood, Rebecca Roeser, your illustrations and designs made my imagination come to life! I'm so grateful for your talent and willingness to make this a reality.

Thank you to Jeanne Roeser for your beautiful calligraphy.

Many thanks to my editor, Shayleen Smith, for your imagination, editing, and love of new worlds.

My childhood best friend, Kristen Stewart. Thank you for creating memories with me that still inspire me.

And for Gabby, Emma, Chloe, Annalee, Selah, Eleana, and Taylor for being my first fans. Each of you will bring glory to the kingdom.

About the Author

Annie Cribbs lives in Colorado Springs, CO with her husband, Ricky, and son, Levi. She's surrounded by mountains but dreams of the ocean. Her love for writing comes from a desire to inspire, encourage, and be a light to young girls. This will be her first book of many.

https://www.facebook.com/Thecrownofilyor
https://www.instagram.com/author_anniecribbs